Everyday Magic

Jess Kidd wanted to be a writer before she could even write. She comes from a big noisy (and nosy) family where storytelling was a favourite pastime. Jess was quite shy when she was little so she learnt to write down the stories she imagined. Then she gave them to her friends and relatives to enjoy.

Jess has received praise for her books and always aims to give her readers an 'experience.' She is currently writing her fourth novel, teaching at her local college and working on TV and film projects. Oh, and playing tug-of-war over socks with Wilkie the dog.

@JessKiddHerself | jesskidd.com

Everyday Magic

JESS KIDD

CANONGATE

First published in Great Britain in 2021 by Canongate Books Ltd,
14 High Street, Edinburgh EH1 1TE

canongate.co.uk

1

Copyright © Jess Kidd, 2021

The right of Jess Kidd to be identified as the
author of this work has been asserted by her in accordance
with the Copyright, Designs and Patents Act 1988

British Library Cataloguing-in-Publication Data
A catalogue record for this book is available on
request from the British Library

ISBN 978 1 83885 020 3

Typeset in Sabon by Palimpsest Book Production Ltd,
Falkirk, Stirlingshire

Printed and bound in Great Britain by Clays Ltd, Elcograf S.p.A.

For Eva

Contents

CHAPTER 1

Out for Delivery

Alfie Blackstack wasn't surprised to find himself an orphan.

His parents had always been careless.

His mother, Mrs Blackstack, was a zookeeper who made the mistake of teasing a hungry lion by dancing through his cage wrapped in a chain of sausages. She did it for a bet.

Grin. Crunch. Slobber. No more Mother.

At the time, little Alfie (oh, just five years old!) still had a father.

Alfie's father, Mr Blackstack, was an ornithologist: he studied birds. Mr Blackstack especially loved angry, sharp-beaked, flappy birds. Furious, vicious birds that hated ornithologists and lived in dangerous, remote places, like slippery cliff faces, scary sea caves and the top of very, very tall trees.

Alfie wasn't brave or daring like his parents. He was scared of lots of things but most especially big cats, vicious birds, high-up places and impatient fathers.

Which was unfortunate, as Mr Blackstack grew impatient around small, timid, trembling children.

Mr Blackstack stopped taking his son on expeditions.

Alfie was relieved. But he was also a bit sad because he knew the reason why his father left him behind. It was because he wasn't daring enough, or strong enough, or good enough. Alfie had, of course, no wish to go to *dangerous* places, but that didn't mean he wouldn't have liked to have seen some nice safe sights: a gentle waterfall perhaps, or calm and friendly monkeys.

On the fateful day that Alfie became an orphan, Mr Blackstack had gone off in a leaky boat, with binoculars, a loaf of bread and a notebook. He was going to a rocky island in the middle of a large choppy ocean to count the birds that lived there.

Mr Blackstack didn't come back.

Police officers, teachers, the local newsagent and neighbours all scratched their heads. What was to be done about Alfie? Orphaned at the start of the summer holidays?

They asked Clarice the childminder. Hadn't she looked after Alfie whenever his father was off on his birdwatching excursions? And didn't Alfie enjoy staying with her (apart from the fish-paste sandwiches she mistakenly thought he loved)? But sadly Clarice hadn't the time or the space to offer Alfie a forever home.

Mr Blackstack's solicitor had the answer. Mr Blackstack had two sisters who lived out in the country. Alfie had aunts.

The aunts were contacted: of course they would take Alfie! Pleasure! Honoured! Thrilled! Pack him up and send him down!

So, Alfie Blackstack was out for delivery:

ORPHAN: small for his age (nine), mouse-brown hair, spectacles, too-big shoes, too-short trousers and an anorak (bright orange). Always. Even in summer.

SUITCASE: filled with ORPHAN's belongings. Among them: his father's spare binoculars, a photograph of his mother with her arm around a panther, and a fish-paste sandwich for the journey.

Alfie looked out of the window as the car sped along. At rain, fields, trees, rain, bushes, cows, rain, farmhouse, wet hens, rain, sad horses, fields.

Clarice the childminder gripped the steering wheel and squinted at the road ahead. She'd forgotten her driving glasses and couldn't see past the end of her nose. Her long silver earrings bounced as the car rocked through potholes and ditches. There was a chicken nugget in the cup holder and jam smeared on the dashboard. Along the back seat there was a line of kids in baby seats cheerfully smacking each other on the head.

Alfie remembered riding in the back of Clarice's car when he was small. It was a warm fuzzy memory. Before school came along and the jostling and jeering and the dread of the playground, because doesn't break time last a hundred years when you've no one to talk to?

Clarice had picked Alfie up from school too, of course. He'd walk out of the gate alone while the other kids raced out roaring or pottered along chatting. Clarice would give him a cheese straw and a sympathetic pat on the arm. She tried her best, really, but sometimes this made Alfie feel worse.

Today they had driven for what felt like a thousand miles. They had listened to *Rock Babies' Nursery Rhymes* for hours. One baby had been sick and Clarice had sworn twice.

Clarice smiled grimly. 'We're making good time; won't be long now. Your aunts will be so looking forward to seeing you!'

'I doubt that,' said Alfie.

'Oh, Alfie! What a thing to say!'

'Before last Thursday I didn't know I had aunts,' Alfie explained. 'I've never even met them. They obviously don't want to be bothered with a nephew.'

'I'm sure that's not the case!' Clarice exclaimed. 'And maybe you just forgot you had aunts?'

Alfie shook his head. 'Having aunts is the sort of thing I would remember.'

Then Alfie did remember: once upon a time, his parents whispering in the kitchen. His parents often whispered in the kitchen when they were alive.

Only this time his mother was doing more than

whispering; she was *hissing*, just like one of those lesser-spotted killer river geese his father was fond of.

'Have you forgotten the *turkey bewitchment*, Phineas?' Alfie's mother hissed to Alfie's father. 'Don't you remember, the boy's first Christmas, when your sisters came to visit?'

'Araminta,' said Alfie's father in a low, angry voice. 'If anything happens to us, my sisters will be the boy's only living relatives. I'm just as flummoxed by that fact as you are, but there it is. Unless you can produce any family members who might give a home to the boy in the unlikely event that we both meet with sticky ends?'

Alfie had hesitated at the doorway.

'That turkey, Phineas, had been roasting *for hours* in the oven!' Alfie's mother's face wore an expression of horror. 'Before it began to move . . .'

Mr Blackstack had looked at Alfie and coughed.

Mrs Blackstack, not noticing Alfie (why would she when he was four and small?), continued. 'Dead as a doornail, brought to life to hop – no – to *dance* across the lunch table—'

'Enough, dearest!' Mr Blackstack had growled, pointing at Alfie. 'The boy.'

Mrs Blackstack glanced at Alfie. Then she turned and glowered down her spoon-billed nose at Mr Blackstack.

'Perhaps he ought to meet his aunts,' she muttered. 'Then he'll know what sort of a *weirdo* family he belongs to.'

'I have aunts?' Alfie asked. The only relatives he knew of were Mum and Dad.

'That's none of your business,' snapped his father.

'But Mum just said . . .'

Mr Blackstack glared at Mrs Blackstack. 'See what you've done.'

'We'll have no more talk of aunts, Alfie,' said Mrs Blackstack coolly. 'Not in this house.'

Then Alfie remembered *another* time when, having sneaked down for a late-night snack, he overheard this from the kitchen:

'I worry about the boy!' Mrs Blackstack was bleating. 'Not to be brave or strong or daring – how will he protect himself out there in the big wide world?'

Alfie had just started school. He spent most days trying to hide from the teachers and other pupils, behind the coats in the cloakroom, or in the toilets, or huddled in an empty corridor. Alfie was always found and led back to class to the smirks and giggles of the other children.

'Spells?' suggested Mr Blackstack.

'Don't bring your family into this again! Your dreadful sisters! Witches the pair of them!'

'I said spells. *You're* the one bringing up my sisters!' He let out a long sigh. 'I left that life behind when I was not much older than Alfie, you know that!'

'All right,' came Mrs Blackstack's reply. 'So, let's talk about Alfie – about how he would survive without bravery, strength or—'

'Perhaps we should just let Alfie stay in his bedroom,' interrupted Mr Blackstack. 'If that's what he really wants to do.'

'But what about *friends*? Ought Alfie not go out and make one at least?'

Mr Blackstack let out a long sigh. 'I think Alfie just likes to be alone.'

Motherless, fatherless, friendless Alfie watched the one lone chicken nugget jiggling in the cup holder with every bump in the road.

He felt just as small and adrift.

He might as well have a label on him. If he had, it would read:

Property of:
Miss Gertrude & Miss Zita Blackstack
Switherbroom Hall
The Back of Beyond

Clarice drove with her nose an inch from the windscreen. 'She sounded really nice on the phone, your Auntie Gertrude.'

Alfie pointed ahead. 'Sheep.'

'Good man.' Clarice swerved to avoid a muddy bundle of sheep by the side of the road. 'She told me that they live in a big draughty house with no electricity in the middle of a forest. Your aunts run a chemist's shop in a village where nothing much happens.'

'Great,' said Alfie, who didn't feel great about anything.

But when he thought about what Clarice had just told him, a hopeful thought glimmered. (There's always a hopeful thought in there somewhere if you look hard enough.)

Alfie had been worried that his aunts would also enjoy dangerous living (slippery cliff faces and flappy fly-in-your-face birds, that sort of thing). But now he knew that they lived in a village where nothing much happened. They ran a chemist's shop. That didn't sound very dangerous.

Was it possible?

Could it be possible?

That his life would be *better* with his aunts?

Then Alfie felt bad. Life hadn't been *awful* at home in London. It was true that he hadn't seen much of his father, but Alfie didn't mind being left alone, not really.

'Aunt Gertrude is doing up a room for you,' Clarice said. 'She asked what you eat and I said mostly pizza and she said would rat casserole do? She sounds like a hoot!' The childminder laughed like a drain.

Alfie looked out of the window; the landscape was growing gloomier. The houses stood further and further apart, as if they didn't like each other. Trees stooped, bushes shivered, crows flew backwards in the blustery rain.

In the back of the car, the babies fell asleep one by one. They snored softly, lulled by the whirr of wet windscreen wipers.

Alfie watched the raindrops blur across the glass.

CHAPTER 2

The Orphan Arrives

Blackstacks' Chemist's Shop stood right in the middle of the village of Little Snoddington. There was not much to the village – only one main road and a duck pond. Most people drove straight through Little Snoddington, even if they were looking for it. Blink and you'd miss it.

It was a place where nothing much happened and the villagers were glad about that. It was also a place where everyone liked to know one another's business. In Little Snoddington, your neighbours would peer over your hedge, or glance into your shopping basket and wonder what you were having for breakfast.

Apart from the chemist's shop, there was a post office and a general store and a tea room where the village went to eat cake and gossip. The vicar and Mrs Vicar lived up the hill near the old church, where jumble sales were held every Saturday and mice played all week round.

Brightly painted cottages gathered close by the main street. They were the plump sort with straw roofs and cosy corners and gardens full of flowers. The villagers liked to compete for the Best Garden prize at the Summer Fair.

Further out of the village were farmhouses set among fields. The farmhouses had fewer flowers and more chickens and pigs. Further out still, through a dark and creepy forest, was Switherbroom Hall, Alfie's new home.

But before we go there, let's visit Blackstacks' Chemist's Shop!

It was always a neat shop, but on the day of Alfie's arrival the shelves had been dusted and the floor swept and the bottles polished.

Gertrude Blackstack was tidy too. Which was unusual.

Her shock of hair, purple that day, had been carefully brushed. She had put on her best shoes (which were gold and made for dancing, but that hardly mattered) and her white chemist's coat was spotless. Zita Blackstack looked the same as she did every day in her dreary black dress and black boots with her black hair in a tight plait.

They stood together behind the counter. Gertrude was watching the rain. Zita was watching a black bat the size of a tea tray fly around the shop. The fat ginger cat curled up in the window was also keeping a sleepy eye on it.

'So, the boy knows nothing about all this?' Zita waved her hands.

'Bats? Chemist's shops?' Gertrude asked.

Zita winced as the bat collided with a shelf. A bottle toppled and fell, but then, just before it hit the ground, it stopped and began to float gently upwards.

Zita glanced at her sister. Gertrude was muttering something under her breath, her eyes fixed on the bottle.

Gertrude's eyes followed the bottle until it floated up onto the shelf and wobbled back into place among the other bottles, all in one piece.

'Spells,' Zita said. 'Magic of the everyday sort that stops bottles falling.'

'Our brother didn't want Alfie learning magic.'

'And neither did Alfie's ghastly mother.'

Gertrude looked at her sister. 'That dancing Christmas turkey didn't help, Zita.'

Zita laughed. It wasn't a nice laugh. 'Oh, the look on her face! The turkey hopping and prancing! Kicking up its roasted legs!'

'Scaring Alfie – he was only a baby!'

'Fat little thing! Quivering in his high chair, eyes all wide!'

'Poor Alfie,' said Gertrude.

'Poor Alfie, my foot!' exclaimed Zita. 'Let's hope he's grown out of being a quivering jelly!'

The bat landed on a hat stand, swung upside down and folded its wings, spying out of the gap between them with glowing red eyes.

Zita grinned at her bat. 'We'll give him something to quiver about, won't we, Magnus?'

'Don't you go scaring the boy!' Gertrude scolded. 'He won't be accustomed to our ways and magic can be a bit worrying when you're not used to it.'

Zita rolled her eyes. 'Especially if you're a scaredy-jelly.'

Gertrude turned down the corners of her mouth. 'Now, you agreed, Zita, that we'll break the news to Alfie gently. You know, about spells and potions and all that.'

'And all that.'

'Show him that magic can be quite delightful.'

Zita narrowed her eyes. 'Pah!'

'And hardly ever involves turning people into frogs or turnips or what have you.'

'All the fun stuff, you mean,' Zita mumbled.

'He's an orphan. The boy is probably sad and frightened and feeling all alone. He won't remember us. We must do our best to make him feel welcome.'

Zita made a rude noise and trundled into the back room to mix up more medicines, the bat flapping behind her.

'And make sure that Familiar of yours behaves himself!' shouted Gertrude. 'Nasty old bat!'

A word on Familiars, if you don't mind, before we get on with the story.

In case you don't know, though I'm sure you do, a Familiar is a witch's sidekick . . . and yes, Alfie's aunts were, in fact, witches.

Bat-owning-cat-loving-cauldron-stirring-spell-casting-wart-growing *witches*.

Only, neither of them had warts really.

But they both had Familiars.

A Familiar is a witch's buddy, her bestie – her furry, feathery, scaly, slithery or spiky partner in crime. A witch and her Familiar go *everywhere* together. They share a bath, a pillow and even the last biscuit. Witches come in all shapes and sizes and ages and so too do Familiars. There are farty, warty, cackling witches as well as smiling, twinkle-eyed, helpful witches. There are baboon and beetle Familiars and there are swan and rabbit Familiars.

It's a tough job being a Familiar. A Familiar has to help out with all their witch's schemes – good or evil.

The right witch picks you – congratulations, a magical life!

Get chosen by the wrong witch and your days will be filled with backfiring spells and smoking cauldrons.

A Familiar will also grow to look like their witch (and vice versa).

Take Alfie's aunts.

Gertrude Blackstack's Familiar was a cat called Rafferty. Rafferty had a marmalade coat and amber eyes. He was the cat curled up in the window of Blackstacks' Chemist's Shop. Rafferty was a cosy cuddle of a cat. He'd twitch his whiskers at the customers and roll over purring, inviting a tickle.

Gertrude and Rafferty had wide smiles and round bellies. They loved people, fireside chairs and dozing.

Zita Blackstack's Familiar was a bat called Magnus. With a fang-filled face and flappy wings that were all skin and spikes, he looked like a broken umbrella.

Magnus liked to spend his days hanging from the hat-stand in the mixing room at the back of the shop. This was where Zita made all the ointments and pills, medicines and powders that Gertrude sold.

Zita and Magnus loved bad weather, bad luck and bad spells. But they hated children.

As you can imagine, Zita and Magnus were especially sour on the day Alfie was due to arrive.

To make matters worse, the shop bell had been tinkling since early morning with customers popping in to see if the newcomer had arrived.

In the shop window, above the display of bandages and bum tonics, zit creams and plasters, a big sign was pasted up. Splattery blue letters read:

WELCOME, ALFRED BLACKSTACK

Rafferty, in his usual spot in the window, was keeping an amber eye out. He looked up at the sign and purred with pride. It was his best work. He caught his blue-paint-tipped tail in his paws and gave it a loving gnaw.

★

As soon as Clarice stopped the car engine, the babies in the back woke up and started howling. Alfie woke up too. He opened his eyes and nearly hit the ceiling in horror.

Squashed against the other side of the window was a face.

14

A nose: mashed, pig-like.

Eyes: wide and staring.

Hair: a frothing purple frizz.

The face pulled away laughing. Alfie cautiously wound the window down.

'I'm Gertrude. Delighted to meet you, Alfie!' She paused. 'Or do you prefer Alfred?'

Alfie attempted a smile. 'If you don't mind, I prefer Alfie.'

'Alfie it is then.' Gertrude smiled back.

Alfie felt a pang of sadness. Only his mother and father had ever called him Alfred. Usually when they were cross with him. Perhaps no one would ever call him Alfred again.

Clarice took Alfie's suitcase from the boot and handed it to Gertrude. Then she kissed Alfie goodbye.

'Best of luck, Alfie,' she whispered. 'I'll come and visit you when you're settled in.'

Alfie had a sinking feeling as he watched Clarice drive away. One of the babies gave him a sticky-handed wave. At the corner of the road Clarice tooted and was gone.

The fat ginger cat begun to nuzzle Alfie's suitcase; he would give it his fish-paste sandwich later.

'Well now, Alfie,' said Gertrude. 'We've a quiet after-noon ahead of us. Uneventful, boring even. It's not very exciting around here, I'm afraid.'

Alfie's heart gladdened for all of one moment; then the shop door opened and out stalked an alarming figure in black. Tall, thin and scowling, with what looked like a large wet dishcloth flying above her.

She stomped towards the black bicycle propped against a nearby lamppost.

'Make no sudden movements,' Gertrude murmured to Alfie. 'Your Aunt Zita is not in the best of moods.'

Zita took hold of the handlebars of the bike. The wet dishcloth darted up to hang from the top of the lamppost.

Alfie pointed to it. 'What *is* that?'

'A bat,' said Gertrude.

'Wow,' replied Alfie, with the definite feeling the bat was scowling down at him. 'I didn't know bats could be that big.'

Zita looked at Alfie. It was a look as cold as a bucket of ice cubes.

Alfie shivered.

'I knew it!' exclaimed Zita. 'He's still a quivering jelly!'

'Remember your manners!' Gertrude scolded. 'Say "how-do-you-do" to the boy.'

'I'd rather pickle him.' Zita jumped on her bicycle and pedalled off down the road.

'No more pickling of children!' Gertrude shouted after her. 'You promised, Zita!'

The bat swooped down from the lamppost to dance in the sky like an inky black kite. It looped a fluttery loop, then zoomed after Zita.

'The bat is *following* her,' said Alfie in amazement.

Gertrude nodded. 'Magnus is her . . . pet.'

'Who has a pet *bat*?'

Gertrude shrugged. 'It's a long story. Let's get you settled in first.'

'She wants to pickle me.'

'She didn't mean it, Alfie.'

'She looked like she meant it.' Alfie found himself strangely upset. 'She doesn't want me here.'

He willed himself not to cry. Not that he ever did. At least not since he was smaller.

'Alfie, *we* are delighted that you are here,' said Gertrude. 'Aren't we, Rafferty?'

The cat wound himself around Alfie's legs and fell over purring on the pavement, inviting a stroke of his warm ginger belly.

Alfie felt very slightly better.

CHAPTER 3

Mrs Mention's Tea Room

Blackstacks' Chemist's Shop was astonishing. It was more like a museum than a shop, with its glass cabinets and old bottles and packets.

Curiously, it seemed far bigger inside than it appeared from the outside.

'Your shop looks very old,' said Alfie to his aunt.

Gertrude nodded. 'It's been here for about a hundred years, so it's older than you and me and Zita put together. Assuming you're still nine?'

Alfie nodded. He looked at Gertrude closely. It was difficult to say how old she was, but she seemed much younger than his father, who always wore suits and looked serious. When Gertrude took off her chemist's coat, he saw that everything she wore was colourful, like a kids' TV presenter.

'I like your anorak,' she smiled. 'It's very orange.'

Alfie knew that if someone says something nice to you it's polite to say something nice back.

'I like your hair. It's very purple.'

'Today it is. Do nine-year-olds eat sandwiches?'

'As long as they are not fish-paste ones,' replied Alfie.

'What about cream cakes?'

'Definitely. Nine-year-olds eat cream cakes.'

'Marvellous. Then we shall go to Mrs Mention's famous tea room.' Gertrude spoke to the cat. 'Lock up, Rafferty, there's a good fellow.'

The cat jumped up onto the counter and hooked a key with the end of its tail. Gertrude pointed at the shelves: the bottles and packets shuffled neatly back in line. She pointed at the blinds: they rolled themselves down.

Alfie closed his eyes, rubbed them and opened them.

He turned to his aunt. 'Did I really just see all that?'

Gertrude laughed, her brown eyes twinkling. 'There'll be time to have a proper look around the shop tomorrow.' She grabbed his suitcase. 'Come on.'

Alfie watched in fascination as the cat strolled after her with the key wound in his tail.

Mrs Mention's Tea Room was world famous because Mrs Mention was an artist in pastry and cakery. She was also one of Gertrude's regular customers (for Blackstacks' Moustache-Minimising Treatment for Ladies). From the outside the tea room looked like a strawberry meringue. The bricks were painted creamy white and there were pink curtains at the window.

Being the afternoon, Mrs Mention's Tea Room was full of old ladies. Some of the old ladies waved at Gertrude and some pretended they hadn't seen her.

Gertrude took a seat, ordering Mrs Mention's Deluxe Cream Tea for Four and a kipper for the cat. The cat jumped up on the chair next to Alfie and winked at him.

Gertrude smiled at Alfie. 'So, now tell me about yourself.'

'I didn't imagine it, did I?' he whispered. 'In the shop, the bottles and packets moved and the blinds closed themselves.'

'No, you didn't imagine it. Poor Alfie! Your parents didn't care for magic much.'

'But there's no such thing as magic!'

'Keep your voice down, Alfie! The whole tea room doesn't have to know.' Gertrude continued quietly, 'Of course there is such a thing as magic. We use spells, mixtures and so forth.'

'Spells, mixtures . . . *potions,* do you mean?'

'Potions – exactly! See, you even know magical words.'

'But don't . . . *witches* make potions?'

'They do. But most of the time they rely on a wonderful pre-made preparation called All-Purpose Witching Powder. Strong enough for most everyday magic.'

'Are you—?'

'I am,' laughed Gertrude.

'I overheard Mum calling you and Aunt Zita . . .' Alfie stopped and blushed.

'Witches? And you thought she was just being rude?'

Alfie nodded. He looked around – everything seemed quite normal in here.

He pointed at the other customers in the tea room. 'So, are they witches too?'

'Nope, they're villagers.'

'But they know about magic?'

'Of course not!' exclaimed Gertrude. 'They're ordinary people!'

'Definitely not witches?'

'It's very difficult to be a witch, Alfie. You need to learn about spells and potions. Then you put the words and mixtures together with a sprinkle of imagination and . . . BAM!'

'Wow . . . I think,' said Alfie.

'Let me demonstrate.'

Gertrude reached into her pocket and brought out a tiny silver bottle. 'Pay attention, now.'

Alfie leant forward.

'A dusting of All-Purpose Witching Powder,' said Gertrude, and shook green powder from the bottle over the bowl of sugar lumps in the centre of the table. Then she muttered something.

Alfie watched with wonder as the sugar lumps began to twitch, shake and then burst, one by one, into perfect sugary flower shapes.

'They're edible, try them!' urged Gertrude.

Alfie picked one up and marvelled at it. Each white petal was edged with green. He took a nibble.

It tasted of sugar, nothing else. But when he looked again the flower had gone and he was holding only a plain square sugar lump. The lump began to twitch again. Alfie saw, at the centre, a black shape wriggling – a fly was trapped inside!

The sugar lump buzzed angrily.

'Ugh!' Alfie dropped it in disgust.

Gertrude laughed. 'You see, Alfie, magic *is* real. It's just that most people don't notice even when it happens right before their eyes.'

Alfie looked around him. She was right: the customers hadn't noticed a thing! They were too busy gobbling cake or slurping soup or gossiping.

'I'll show you,' said Gertrude.

She tipped more green powder from the bottle into the palm of her hand and blew it into the air.

On a nearby table, the rock buns grew beetle legs and scampered around the cake stand. As a lady poured hot tea, the steam swirled from the teapot spout a fantastic glittery green. She stopped pouring and looked into her cup.

'She's seen it! The green steam!'

'Wait, watch,' whispered Gertrude.

The customer sniffed and turned back to her crossword.

'Aside from *noticing* magic,' murmured Gertrude. 'There's one more thing that makes ordinary people different to not-so-ordinary people.'

22

'What is it?'

'They don't believe in magic. If you do believe – from your toenails to your hair-tips – magic will work! We use magic every day.'

'To tidy up a shop?' suggested Alfie.

'Exactly!'

'Or make a cat wink?'

'Oh, there's no magic there. Rafferty does that all by himself, don't you, Raffy?'

The cat winked again.

Alfie thought a moment. 'About magic—'

'All in good time, Alfie,' answered Gertrude. 'Magic is rather tricky and a tea room is not the best place to learn about it.'

A lady the size of a wardrobe in a flowery apron sailed towards their table with a tray. She set down a teapot.

'Is that your nephew, Gertrude?'

'Yes, Mrs Mention, this is Alfie.'

Mrs Mention leaned in closer to Alfie. 'This is a *nice* village; we don't like any trouble here. Are *you* a trouble-maker?'

'I don't think so.'

Mrs Mention brought her mouth, pink with thick lipstick, level with his ear. 'I'd steer clear of Auntie Zita if I were you. She hates children, especially troublemakers. Auntie Zita knows how to deal with troublemakers.' She picked up a butter knife and drew it across her throat, pirate style.

Alfie startled.

Gertrude frowned. 'Mrs Mention, the news, if you please.'

'The circus has arrived,' reported Mrs Mention sourly. 'They've been spotted on the edge of town.'

Gertrude looked delighted. 'A week early – wonderful!'

From Mrs Mention's expression Alfie could tell *she* didn't think it was wonderful news at all.

'Will you and your sister be letting the *circus people* use your field again this year?' Mrs Mention asked Gertrude.

Mrs Mention said the words *circus people* as you would say the words *sticky dog poo*.

'Of course,' nodded Gertrude.

Mrs Mention raised one eyebrow. 'After what happened *last year*?'

Rafferty stopped pawing the tablecloth and glanced at Gertrude.

Gertrude looked defiant. 'Yes.'

'What happened last year?' asked Alfie, intrigued. He had never been to a circus before.

'Last year the human cannonball crashed through the roof of the school, and the acrobat formation team – who are, in fact, goats – ate the vicar's underpants from the rectory washing line. Then the big top caught on fire,' said Mrs Mention bitterly.

'No way!' exclaimed Alfie.

'The fire-breathing dragon-lady had the hiccups, apparently.' Mrs Mention pointed out of the window. 'Speak of the devils. Here comes trouble!'

24

Outside, all along the road, brightly painted buses and vans and caravans were passing by, honking their horns loudly. Children and dogs ran alongside.

Mrs Mention scowled. 'Why can't people live in houses and have proper jobs?'

'They do have a proper job – they run a circus!' Gertrude replied.

Mrs Mention shook her head. 'Living in *buses*, I ask you. Not a bathroom in sight.'

'Mrs Mention, the world would be very boring if everyone lived in a bungalow and ran a tea room.'

Mrs Mention stuck her nose in the air and sailed off between the tables.

Gertrude nudged Alfie. 'Oh, marvellous day! You *and* the circus arrive in town!'

A tall girl ducked out from the circus crowd and into Mrs Mention's Tea Room. Rafferty bounced onto the table, his tail held high with happiness.

'Calypso!' shouted Gertrude.

'Gertrude! Rafferty!' cried the girl.

She flew across the room, her fair hair in a messy ponytail. She picked up the cat and squeezed him.

'Meet my nephew,' said Gertrude. 'Alfie's the exact same age as you – so you must be friends!'

Alfie felt his cheeks turn red.

Calypso looked at Alfie.

Alfie looked away. He was suddenly aware of his too-big shoes and too-short trousers. Of his spectacles and his anorak.

At least it had rained a bit today.

Because even on the hottest summer's day Alfie wore an anorak; he liked having the pockets and pulling the hood up and pretending he was invisible. Which he wasn't, of course, because his anorak was bright orange, so bright he could probably be seen from space.

Alfie, in other words, was suddenly aware of all the things that made other kids tease him at school.

'All right, Alfie?' said Calypso.

Alfie glanced up at her.

Calypso was *smiling* at him.

He was so surprised he smiled back.

'You there, circus girl!' cried Mrs Mention. 'Get out! Out! Out!'

Calypso fished a pile of flyers from the front of her sweatshirt. She passed one to Alfie and waved the rest at Mrs Mention.

'Can I leave these?'

'Advertise your rotten show here?' barked Mrs Mention. 'I think not!'

'Ah, go on!'

'Hop it. I will not have circus people in my tea room!'

Calypso pulled a face and skipped out of the door.

A gaggle of clowns romped past the window, walking on their hands. They tapped on the tea-room window with the toes of their huge silly shoes. A circus pony paused to nuzzle the flowerpots on Mrs Mention's windowsills.

Some of the customers laughed, until Mrs Mention turned her glare on them.

Alfie looked at the flyer in his hand: crazy clowns and rowdy ponies, trapeze artists and daredevil bikers, a fire-breathing dragon-lady and a human cannonball.

FAGAN'S FAMILY CIRCUS
FOR ALL THE FAMILY!

Alfie rushed to the window. Calypso was heading down the road with the others. She did a cartwheel past the butcher's shop. Then she looked back and waved at Alfie, who ducked behind the curtain.

When he looked again, Calypso was gone.

CHAPTER 4

The Dusty Doorknob

After cream cakes, sandwiches (*not* fish-paste) and three pots of tea, Gertrude suggested they should go home.

With the circus parade long gone, the village was as quiet as Sunday.

Gertrude stopped outside a shop along the lane. 'We'll pop in here, Alfie, for a few supplies.'

It was a narrow, tatty-looking shop, squeezed between two much smarter neighbours. The windows were cobwebbed and the sign that swung above the door had no name but a curious picture of a weasel holding a balloon.

It looked as if no one had been inside for years.

'What is this place?' asked Alfie.

'Mr Fingerhut's Fun Emporium.'

28

Mr Fingerhut's Fun Emporium was a dusty muddle of a shop. Anything and everything seemed to be on sale, from fancy-dress costumes to water pistols, roller skates to white mice in silver cages.

Gertrude stepped up to the counter. 'Mr Fingerhut, I'd like to order a bumper pack of fun boys' games.'

Mr Fingerhut shuffled off through a door at the back of the shop muttering to himself darkly. Alfie was trying to think of a way to explain that he wasn't a fun boy at all when Mr Fingerhut returned carrying several tatty boxes of jigsaws and an old chess set.

Mr Fingerhut put the games down on the counter, then peered over the edge at Alfie. 'And what is that?'

On a shelf behind Mr Fingerhut, a stuffed weasel on a wooden stand was also staring at Alfie. The weasel had black beady eyes and was very lifelike.

Alfie felt uncomfortable at being examined so closely. 'My nephew, Alfie Blackstack,' said Gertrude.

'Bit on the small side for a Blackstack, isn't he?' Mr Fingerhut rang the order through an ancient till. 'What age?'

'Alfie is nine,' answered Gertrude frostily, rummaging in her purse. 'And he's just the right size.'

Mr Fingerhut took the money and dropped it in the till.

Gertrude put the games in her shopping bag and wandered off to rummage in a bucket marked DISCOUNTED FUN. It seemed to be full of joke glasses and feathery headdresses.

Mr Fingerhut turned to Alfie. 'Here, boy,' he said in a

low voice. 'Are you aware that there's no electricity up at your aunts' house?'

'Sort of.'

'No computer, no phone, no television,' smirked Mr Fingerhut. 'You'll need to find other ways to amuse yourself.'

'Great,' said Alfie quietly.

Mr Fingerhut reached under the counter and produced a small, very dusty box.

'Free gift.' He tapped the lid with a long yellow fingernail. 'Extra jollity.'

'What is it?'

Mr Fingerhut wiped the dust from the box with the end of his beard. 'Doorknob.'

'You're giving me a doorknob?' said Alfie.

'Missing its door. Can't sell a doorknob without a door.' Mr Fingerhut took the dusty object from the box and held it out to Alfie. 'It's yours.'

Alfie took it. 'Thanks. I think.'

The old shopkeeper's mouth twitched with merriment inside his dirty white beard. On the shelf behind him, the stuffed weasel seemed to be having an attack of the hiccups.

'Have you met your Aunt Zita yet?'

Alfie nodded.

The old man looked sympathetic. 'I'll let you into a secret: that doorknob ain't a doorknob.'

'It isn't?' asked Alfie.

Mr Fingerhut held a gnarly finger to his lips. 'Shh, keep

that to yourself. Your aunts might not like you having too much fun. And if they find out about this doorknob which ain't a doorknob, well, you didn't get it from me, understand?'

Alfie looked at the object in his hand, suddenly fearful. 'I don't want to take something that's going to get me into trouble.'

'Nonsense! It's just something to help you pass the time in that draughty old house with no computers and your crabby Aunt Zita. Bring a little *magic* into your unfortunate young life. Orphan, ain't you?'

'Yes, but . . .' Alfie looked closely at the old man. 'What do you mean by *magic*?'

'They bring out that green powder, then . . . POP!'

Alfie startled. 'My aunt said no one else here in the village knew about magic!'

'Did she now?' Mr Fingerhut grinned. It wasn't a nice grin.

'She said that people don't notice it.'

'Some do, some don't.'

Alfie frowned at the doorknob. 'What is it?'

'You work it out. You're a Blackstack, ain't you?' The old man looked at Alfie slyly. 'Blackstacks are supposed to be *clever*.'

Alfie slipped the doorknob into his pocket, hoping he wouldn't regret it.

Mr Fingerhut glanced over at Gertrude. Alfie's aunt was trying on a red glittery top hat and a large false moustache.

31

'Will you be letting the circus use your field again this year, Miss Blackstack?'

Gertrude squinted over her bushy moustache. 'That's no business of yours, Ignatius Fingerhut.'

A smile twitched behind the old man's beard. 'Mrs Mention says that the circus always brings trouble—'

'Oh, I know what Mrs Mention says!' Gertrude blustered. 'Come on, Alfie. Time to go.'

Gertrude swept out of the shop, Rafferty running after her.

Alfie went to follow.

'Welcome to Little Snoddington, Master Blackstack.' The old shopkeeper grinned. 'You're in for a whole world of fun.'

It was getting dark as they took a shortcut through the forest, a narrow winding path. Gertrude dragged Alfie's suitcase along and Alfie did his best to keep up.

The doorknob was surprisingly heavy in his anorak pocket.

He wished he hadn't accepted it from Mr Fingerhut, with his sly look and straggly old beard.

Mr Fingerhut had said that the Blackstacks were clever.

Alfie wrinkled his nose; the Blackstacks were weird more like.

His father had enjoyed searching for nasty birds in dangerous places. Aunt Gertrude made rock cakes scamper and steam turn green and had a winking cat. Aunt Zita had a humongous pet bat and wanted to pickle Alfie.

And magic was *real*.

Nothing was normal any more.

They went through the tall trees, so dark and dripping, although it had stopped raining hours ago. They were the type of trees that have gnarly faces in the trunks. Alfie tried not to look at them too closely.

'Welcome, Alfie!' panted Gertrude. 'Your new home – Switherbroom Hall!'

In a gloomy clearing in the gloomy forest stood a big gloomy house.

It was nothing at all like the smart London townhouse Alfie had left behind.

There was nothing smart about this place.

The roof was crooked and the windows were wonky. Green smoke rose from the chimney and twisted into the sky. Stone steps led up to the front door, which was black.

Alfie felt as if he was being watched, that there were eyes at every one of the many windows. But looking up he saw no one.

Gertrude bumped Alfie's suitcase up the path.

Clumps of moss scuttled out of her way.

The front door opened, all by itself, with a growl.

Alfie thought about running – but where would he run to?

Before him: a scary house.

Behind him: a scary forest.

'Alfie, come inside, quickly!' called Gertrude. 'I've something to show you before the sun sets!'

With one glance back at the trees (which seemed to have grown even taller and were linking branches), Alfie followed his aunt into the house. Through the front door, tripping and crashing down a dark hallway – the house was as cluttered and cobwebby as Mr Fingerhut's shop.

Gertrude opened a door and stepped outside.

What a view!

At the back of the house green fields sloped all the way down to where the forest began again.

In the furthest field, caravans, buses and vans were parked and a fire had been lit.

'The circus!' exclaimed Alfie.

Gertrude nodded. 'Our summertime neighbours. The Fagan Family Circus!'

Alfie thought of the tall circus girl. *Calypso*. He'd never known anyone with a name like that.

She had smiled at him.

Gertrude glanced at the wall light above them and murmured something under her breath. The light sparked and began to shine brightly. It was curiously shaped – like a glow-worm. A fat bug with a bright shining tail!

Alfie watched astonished as, all the way down the hall, lights sparked and shone, each one shaped like a glow-worm.

'They're not . . . *real* bugs, are they?'

But Gertrude had marched off ahead.

Now that the hallway was lit, Alfie could see around

himself properly. Paintings of olden-days people crowded the walls; they seemed to frown down at him. Blood-red carpet ran up the staircase. Alfie noticed with a shudder that the bannister was shaped like a snake. The head of the snake was at the bottom of the stairs, with an open mouth and fangs as long as Alfie's thumb. Its eyes, two ruby stones, glinted.

The rest of the snake staircase twisted very high, through so many floors that Alfie felt dizzy looking up.

'The staircase is mostly friendly,' said Gertrude, 'but I wouldn't recommend sliding down that particular bannister. Although you don't look like the kind of boy who slides down bannisters.'

'I don't?' asked Alfie, a little disappointed.

Gertrude smiled. 'Come and see your room!'

Alfie gingerly followed Gertrude up the staircase.

On every step, there seemed to be a pile of junk: books, strange plants, jars of wizened things and, oddest of all, bits of old vacuum cleaners.

'You have a lot of vacuum cleaners.'

'Best way to get around,' replied Gertrude. 'Mind your step, Alfie.'

The plants tangled at Alfie's ankles and the books toppled as he passed. He kept his eyes on the stairs, for whenever he looked away the objects seemed to rearrange themselves to trip him up.

As Alfie and Gertrude passed, the glow-worm lights lit up and the portraits glowered down.

At least there was no sign of Aunt Zita.

'Is Zita here?' Alfie asked quietly when they reached the top of the stairs.

'No, the lights glow green when she's in.' Gertrude led Alfie along the corridor. 'This is your room.'

Gertrude opened the door.

The glow-worm lights glimmered to life.

Alfie took a deep breath.

This was an *actual* nightmare.

The room was painted dark red with drifty white ghosts sponged on the walls. The ghosts had fangs drawn on in marker pen.

At the side of the room was a lumpy bed. The bed had a red blanket with plastic joke cut-off fingers sewn on it.

Alfie thought of his bedroom back in London: the blue duvet and the blue walls, the television and the games console, the shelves of books and the cosy rug.

His home in London was bright and clean and warm. Home.

This was his home now, this creepy, cobwebby old place, lit by bugs.

'What do you think, Alfie?' asked Gertrude anxiously. 'Don't you like it?'

'It's great.' Alfie managed. 'It's . . . different.'

'Let's go and have dinner. You can unpack later.'

Then Alfie remembered. 'Is it true that there's no TV?'

'Magic makes the picture crackly.'

'And no computer?' asked Alfie.

'Mr Fingerhut gave us a computer,' said Gertrude brightly.

Alfie felt hopeful. 'He did?'

'It went BANG!'

'Oh,' said Alfie.

'The magic again, I'm afraid,' smiled Gertrude.

The lights began to spark green.

Gertrude's smile disappeared. 'It looks like Zita will be joining us.'

'She doesn't really pickle boys, does she?'

Gertrude laughed nervously. 'Zita can get a bit grumpy. Perhaps avoid talking to her, or looking at her, or drawing her attention in any way.'

That didn't sound too good.

'What about her bat?' asked Alfie.

'Magnus? Oh, he prefers tomato juice to blood these days, so you should be all right. Just watch your eyes.'

'My eyes?'

'It's probably best to keep your glasses on,' warned Gertrude. 'Eyes are a favourite snack of bats.'

'Oh, that's disgusting!' cried Alfie.

'Isn't it?' nodded Gertrude.

There was a bang that shook the whole house. The lights flickered. The plastic fingers on the bedspread waggled.

Gertrude groaned. 'Oh dear. Zita's in an even worse mood than usual.'

Rafferty pawed open the wardrobe and climbed inside.

CHAPTER 5

The Dangers of Doorknobs

Alfie sat very still.

Zita was seated at the head of the kitchen table with a steaming bowl at her elbow. She was reading a newspaper when they walked in and hadn't looked up since. The bat was hanging upside down from the back of her chair. It was even bigger up close and had a ghoulish leathery look about it. Alfie could see the tips of its ears and its horrid pig-mousey face. Thankfully its eyes were closed, the lids wrinkled and grey.

Gertrude crept about the kitchen, opening cupboards and scratching her head.

Rafferty jumped on the table and leant against Alfie's shoulder. Alfie was thankful to have him near.

Alfie wished that he'd taken off his anorak. It was bound to draw Zita's attention, being the brightest colour

38

in the universe. Also, it made a crinkly noise when he moved. He would have to stay very still.

He tried to look around by just moving his eyes.

Pots bubbled on a cooker. The lids of the pots hopped up and down. Now and again the flames crackled green and whizzed and sparked. Alfie heard muttering coming from inside the pots.

Zita got up and wandered over to the cooker. She lifted the lid of a pot and glared inside. The flames flattened and the muttering stopped.

Alfie stole a look at his aunt. Zita had hair the colour of raven wings and eyes the colour of coal lumps. She was stern and so pale she looked as though she was carved out of snow.

The sisters were not a bit alike. Zita wore only black. Gertrude wore just about every colour. Zita was tall and thin. Gertrude was small and round. They were not old, but then they weren't exactly *young*. They certainly seemed younger than Alfie's parents, who had always worn grown-uppish clothes like hats and lace-up shoes and raincoats.

Zita still hadn't looked at him.

She sat down at the table and turned the pages of her newspaper. She poked about in the bowl beside her with a fork. It looked to be stew of some kind, yellowish and thick. Alfie hoped he wouldn't be eating the same.

Zita stabbed the stew and the stew moved.

A slug flopped out of the bowl and onto the table.

Alfie cried out in surprise.

Zita speared the slug and popped it in her mouth. She pointed her fork at Alfie. 'How long is that staying?'

Gertrude, over by the oven, straightened up. '*His* name is Alfie and this is his home now. He's here to stay.'

Zita's stare didn't waver. Alfie felt stabbed by it, like the slug on her fork. She went fishing again, jab, jab. A soft hiss, another slug was done for.

Alfie shuddered and looked away.

Zita's voice was as soft and slippery as satin ribbon. 'Do you know what we are, Alfred Blackstack?'

Alfie could feel Zita's eyes on him.

His brain panicked, looking for the right answer.

'Well?' barked Zita.

What *was* the right answer: *chemists, weirdos, oddly magical aunts . . . witches*?

Even if it was true, it hardly seemed polite to *say* it.

Should Alfie call his newly found relative (who didn't seem to like him much) a *witch*?

Well, *would you*?

'Come on, Alfred,' Zita mocked. 'Spit it out. I *dare* you.'

An incredible thing happened.

A feeling of bravery began to grow inside Alfie – only a speck, mind.

He took a deep breath and raised his eyes to Zita's face.

Her black eyes glittered and her smile was mean.

Alfie's bravery vanished – he daren't speak!

'We're wicked witches,' gloated Zita. 'Didn't your bird-brained father tell you?'

'Zita!' Gertrude exclaimed.

'Or your daft, munched-up mother?' Zita continued. 'She didn't like us much either.'

Alfie couldn't answer. He closed his eyes and wished himself anywhere else, *anywhere* – dangling from a zipline, up a tree, climbing a slippery cliff face. As long as it was far away from Zita's cold, cruel voice.

'Look at me, Alfie. Isn't that true?'

Alfie looked up and froze with horror.

Zita's nose had grown to the size of a marrow. Alfie shuddered to see it ripe with juicy warts.

Her face was no longer as white as snow – it was a ferocious shade of red. Butcher's shop red!

'Zita!' cried Gertrude. 'You're scaring the boy out of his wits!'

'It's only a bit of fun!' replied the terrible red-faced Zita.

Zita's bat hopped up on the tabletop and headed towards Alfie – wing tips tapping, knuckles scrabbling, fangs bared.

Alfie screamed and ran.

Zita's laugh followed right behind him: wicked and gleeful.

Alfie stopped running. He was in yet another hallway with green-glowing wall lights and snooty portraits.

Had he run upstairs or downstairs? What floor was he on? How could he get so easily lost?

Something buzzed in his pocket.

Alfie jumped.

41

It was the doorknob!

He took it out and it stopped buzzing. The doorknob was cobwebbed and filthy. Alfie wiped it on his anorak.

And there, inside the doorknob, was a blizzard: snow-flakes rushing and turning.

Alfie realised this wasn't a doorknob – it was a *snow globe*!

The snow began to settle.

Alfie saw a gloomy house, in a gloomy clearing, surrounded by a gloomy forest. The roof was crooked and the windows were wonky.

It was Switherbroom Hall!

Lights flickered in all the little windows. Alfie watched in amazement as the tiny front door opened and footsteps appeared along the path.

Then, all of a sudden, a face pressed against the glass. A face with a freckled, upturned nose, huge yellow eyes and a shock of bright green hair!

The face gave Alfie a wide, sharp-toothed grin. A finger tapped on the glass.

Alfie dropped the snow globe in fright and turned and ran.

He wanted no more of this!

Witchy aunts.

Scary bat.

Creepy house.

Bug-lights.

Snow globes with faces inside.

ARRGGGGHHHHHHH!

The snow globe overtook him.

Alfie stopped.

The snow globe stopped.

Alfie turned and ran in the other direction.

The snow globe bounced after him, along corridors and down the stairs.

Alfie saw a door open and ducked inside.

He found himself in a library.

It was a library that had more books than Alfie had ever seen. Shelves and shelves and shelves of books!

Alfie looked around himself with wonder; it would take him a hundred years to read all of these books!

Books were discouraged in the Blackstack house unless, of course, they were books about bird-watching or lion taming.

Mr and Mrs Blackstack believed that reading made children lazy and cowardly. Readers skulked on sofas when they should be outside climbing cliffs or trailing tigers. His parents were disappointed when they caught Alfie reading the books he had sneaked from the library. But Alfie couldn't help it if he preferred his adventures in a story.

The snow globe hopped up and down on the toe of Alfie's foot.

'OWW!'

'Shh!' said a deep voice from over near a bookcase.

A very old man drifted across the room with a finger held up to his lips. He wore a faded olden-days dress and bonnet. But what made him really different was the fact that he was *see-through*.

Then Alfie realised the old man was a *ghost*.

A real live ghost!

Should Alfie be scared? If the ghost was a *librarian*: possibly. Librarians could be fierce. Of a *ghost librarian*: definitely.

The ghost pointed a long see-through finger at the snow globe by Alfie's feet. 'Is that your imp, boy?'

Alfie looked down at the snow globe; the creature inside waved up at him. 'That's an imp?'

The ghost peered closely at Alfie. 'Do your aunts know you have this here imp, Alfie Blackstack?'

Alfie's cheeks flushed red. 'Mr Fingerhut gave it to me, sort of a bit in secret.' He paused. 'How do you know my name?'

'Walls have ears,' said the ghost. 'I'd keep this snow globe to yourself if I were you, having taken something you shouldn't.'

'But I didn't want to take it!'

The ghost raised his eyebrows. 'You haven't got off to the best start, have you? Especially with your Aunt Zita.'

'It's her fault – with her face and her bat!'

The ghost laughed, freezing Alfie's hair on end. 'Well, Zita wouldn't take kindly to you keeping an imp trapped in a snow globe; she likes them, goodness knows why, nasty, tricksy creatures!'

'I didn't trap him there!' exclaimed Alfie.

The ghost shrugged. 'You'd be better off dropping him down the nearest well.'

The imp pulled a rude face.

Alfie picked up the snow globe carefully and put it in his anorak pocket, trying to ignore the jabbering imp. 'He chased me here.'

'He wants you to find a book.' The ghost pointed over Alfie's shoulder. 'So does the library.'

Alfie turned to see a cloud of books fluttering behind him like great papery moths.

Nothing in his life was normal now.

Alfie took the books to a nearby chair. The chair was old and gnarly legged, with a seat of green leather, the feet shaped into claws. Alfie sat down. The chair creaked crossly.

The librarian coughed politely. 'I wouldn't sit on that *particular* chair if I were you. There's a less quarrelsome one in the corner there.'

Alfie got up and carried the pile of books to the less quarrelsome chair.

The books were heavy and old and written in a language he didn't understand.

Before long the pile was reduced to one small book he could actually read. It seemed newer than the others and had a picture of a small silver bottle on the cover.

The book was called *Everyday Magic for Beginners*. Alfie opened it and read:

Simple Spells for Youngsters
Curse Your Enemy
Fun with Warts

There were pictures of witches in action: stirring cauldrons, casting spells on their enemies and proudly holding toads.

Alfie turned the pages in wonder.

From what he now read, it seemed that magic was just a load of recipes – ear of bat, toe of newt – and a few words babbled over the mixture and BAM!

There were spells for everything, the book said.

There was a spell for making a five-storey chocolate cake from a carrot. There was a spell for turning a bucket into a submarine.

Then Alfie had a thought.

Couldn't he learn a bit of magic? Becoming invisible to mean cucumber-nosed witches and their killer bats would be a good start.

Because, Alfie thought, sadly, he really had nowhere else to go.

He couldn't live with Clarice – she had babies to mind. His old house in London was closed up now.

He tried to read on, but his eyes had gone all blurry with tears. The tears began to trundle down his cheeks and patter on his anorak. After a while, Alfie took a deep breath and wiped his face with his sleeve. Then he turned another page, looking for a spell that could save him from his Aunt Zita.

CHAPTER 6

Fagan's Family Circus

Alfie woke to the sound of scrabbling at his bedroom door. The handle turned and the door opened.

Rafferty trotted in. Gertrude followed, carrying a tray.

'Knock, knock,' said Gertrude, setting the tray on the dressing table. 'I've brought you some breakfast. I'm sorry Zita scared you away from your dinner.'

'I wasn't that scared,' fibbed Alfie. He found his glasses and put them on.

Gertrude was dressed in rainbow clothes again. Today her hair was pink.

'It was just Zita's idea of a joke, you know,' Gertrude said. 'Slug stew, cucumber snozz.'

'Very funny.'

Gertrude glanced at Alfie. 'We could find you a nice *ordinary* family to live with, if you'd prefer?'

Rafferty flattened his ears. His tail dipped down.

Alfie thought for a moment about what it would be like to live with a nice *ordinary* family. Sunday dinners, TV shows, Saturday football, homework and ironed trousers.

Then he thought about Zita.

And the angry imp in the snow globe in his anorak pocket.

Ordinary would be nice.

Then, quite unexpectedly, he thought of the circus and Calypso.

'I might stick around for a bit, if that's OK?' Alfie said.

Rafferty purred.

Gertrude grinned from ear to ear. 'Goodo. This summer will be FUN, FUN, FUN!'

Alfie headed down to the bottom field pushing a wheelbarrow full of vegetables.

This didn't feel like FUN, FUN, FUN.

The vegetables from Gertrude's garden were really strange. Purple peppers, blue tomatoes and something that looked like a knobbly blood-red radish.

He thought of Zita turning warty and red. Maybe that was her true face.

The wheelbarrow wobbled and some veg fell out. Alfie stopped for the millionth time. He was to deliver Gertrude's creepy-looking garden produce to Mr Fagan as a welcome gift for the circus folk. She had given him a woolly hat to wear, because although it was summer there was a chill to the morning air. Otherwise Alfie had polished his glasses and put on his too-short trousers, too-big shoes and his anorak (with the snow globe safely zipped in the pocket until he dropped it down a well or whatever else he ought to do with it).

Alfie wondered if he could look like any more of a weirdo.

He hoped that Calypso wasn't around.

Then he hoped she was.

She had *smiled* at him.

Maybe they could be friends?

But what if she saw him pushing a barrow full of odd vegetables, wearing his aunt's hat?

Would she want to be friends with him then?

Calypso. It was a great name. He repeated it to himself. *Calypso, Calypso, Calypso.*

It sounded like music.

Alfie took off the woolly hat and stuffed it into his pocket.

He tried not to think about what he looked like.

He tried to think about something else.

Books.

Alfie had sat up reading the book from the library half the night while waiting for Aunt Zita to pickle him.

But the more he found out about magic the less he understood!

He learnt that magic is neither good nor bad: it's as helpful or wicked as those who use it. There were two famous families, the Blackstacks and the Morrows, who once upon a time wrote down all the spells everyone had always used and invented a few more.

Alfie was surprised to learn that his family had been super-important in the witch world.

Each family had their own symbol. The Blackstacks had a raven and the Morrows had a dove. Each family thought themselves the cleverest and best. They had cast spells on each other. They had started wars and fought each other. The Head Witch was always from one or the other of these families. When it was their turn, each family put forward their cleverest, toughest or fiercest witch. It was an important and difficult job. The Head Witch had to boss all the other witches around.

Alfie wondered who the Head Witch might be.

He hoped it wasn't Zita, although he suspected she'd be good at it.

As Alfie neared the circus camp, he forgot all about ravens and doves and Head Witches. Up ahead a gaggle of kids were sitting on a fence.

Alfie felt worried: the kids looked like they might be the teasing kind.

Luckily, they ignored him. They were watching a boy riding a pony around the field.

First, the boy rode with one hand on the reins, then he rode with no hands on the reins, then he knelt on the saddle, then he stood up on the back of the horse.

He had long black hair and wore a black T-shirt.

He was a bit of a show-off.

Even so, Alfie wished he could ride a pony and look tough. But he didn't like horses and Clarice had chosen his clothes. Then a thought struck him: was Calypso watching too? He looked for her.

No Calypso. Alfie could see tents and caravans and buses beyond the field. Calypso must live in one of those.

To the right there was another field.

Alfie looked at the map Gertrude had given him: two fields, one with a big X through it and a drawing of a bull. The bull had fangs. It would probably be some sort of magical bull then. To deliver the vegetables Alfie must cross the field *without* the bull, the field that had pony boy showing off in it.

Alfie opened the gate and pushed his wheelbarrow through. Then he closed the gate behind him – he knew that much about the countryside.

Halfway across the field he heard hooves hitting the ground like a rolling drumbeat. He felt wind on his cheek as the pony whipped by.

The kids along the fence were waving and shouting at Alfie. He couldn't understand what they were saying.

It could be '*move forward*'; it could be '*go back*'.

The pony stopped at the far side and threw back its head. The boy struggled to hold onto the reins.

The pony danced and turned, snorting air. The boy's face reddened.

Alfie ran, unusual vegetables spilling from the wheelbarrow. He reached the gate and pulled at it, but a rope tied it shut.

The children along the fence jeered at Alfie.

Hooves thundered behind him.

Alfie turned and saw horse and boy glaring down at him.

'You startled my horse. I could have fallen!' the boy growled. 'What's wrong with you?'

'Sorry!'

'Apologise to the horse!'

'Sorry, horse,' muttered Alfie.

'Now kiss the horse,' demanded the boy.

The children on the fence roared with laughter.

The boy narrowed his eyes. 'Go on.'

Alfie shook his head. 'I don't want to.'

The boy moved the pony a few steps closer to Alfie. 'I said KISS THE HORSE.'

'LEAVE HIM ALONE!' came a shout.

Alfie looked up to see Calypso on the other side of the gate. She was sticking up for him!

Alfie felt relieved and embarrassed all at once.

The boy turned his pony and rode off across the field, aiming at the fallen vegetables. The pony kicked through them.

Calypso untied the gate. 'Don't mind him. The GREAT TOERAG, Shane Fagan.'

'Thank you,' said Alfie gruffly, his cheeks burning, 'but I had it sorted.'

'You did, of course,' replied Calypso, righting the wheelbarrow, which was lying on its side.

The other kids were nudging each other and laughing at him.

'Just leave them!' he snapped at Calypso, who was gathering up vegetables. 'I can do it!'

'I was only trying to help.'

'I don't want your help!' The words came out far louder and angrier than Alfie meant them to.

Calypso straightened up, surprised.

'Just leave me alone,' said Alfie miserably.

Calypso scowled at him. 'Gladly.'

Alfie watched her go back through the gate. He wanted to run after her and apologise, but he didn't.

He couldn't, with all those awful kids staring and smirking!

Instead he collected up the vegetables and put them back in the wheelbarrow.

The circus folk were up early, chatting and drinking tea, sitting on the steps of caravans.

Alfie would find Mr Fagan, deliver this stuff and get out before any other mishaps occurred.

A man with a big bald head nodded to him from a deckchair. On the side of the man's van was painted:

MICKY MOONY – HUMAN CANNONBALL

He's got the right head for it, thought Alfie unkindly.

Further along, a lady dressed in shiny green scales breathed on a giant cotton bud. The cotton bud burst into flames and she spun it around fast, like a Catherine wheel.

Fire-breathing dragon-lady, Alfie thought.

She waved at him, but he didn't feel like waving back.

The big circus tent was growing like a ginormous mushroom. It was white-and-red-striped, bright in the morning sun. Circus people were tightening ropes and carrying benches inside.

A sandy-haired man with a beard was standing on the back of a truck, giving orders. He beckoned Alfie from the roof of the van. 'Can I help you?'

Alfie parked his wheelbarrow. 'I'm looking for Mr Fagan. My Aunt Gertrude sent these.'

'I'm Tom Fagan.' He smiled, wide and friendly. 'And you are?'

'Alfie Blackstack.'

A white-haired lady with a pipe, who was untangling a rope nearby, glanced up. 'Blackstack you say, boy?'

Alfie nodded.

She wandered over, making a creaking sound as she moved. At first Alfie thought it was the lady's old bones making the noise, for she was a great age. Then he realised it was her leather jacket and trousers.

'This is our daredevil, Granny Fagan,' said Tom. 'She rides the stunt bike.'

Tom pointed to the motorbike parked outside the big top. It was huge and shiny and decorated with sparkling silver stars – just like the stars on Granny Fagan's leather jacket and trousers.

Granny Fagan took out her pipe and squinted at Alfie. 'You look like your father.'

'You knew my father?' asked Alfie in surprise.

'When he was your age,' nodded Granny Fagan. 'I reckon you're less of a rascal.'

Alfie looked at the ground, his eyes a bit watery all of a sudden. He wasn't sure he wanted to talk about his father with these people he didn't know.

'I've never seen a tent so big,' he mumbled.

Tom smiled. 'My daughter, Calypso, is somewhere about. She'd be happy to show you around.'

Alfie doubted that. 'I can look around by myself.'

'Go on then! Only keep your wits about you, Alfie!' warned Granny Fagan.

Alfie went inside the big top. He was careful to keep out of the way while the benches and staging, scaffolding and nets, stairways and ladders were set up.

The workers moved quickly; the huge space was full of people, but everyone had their own job to do and went about it skilfully.

Alfie couldn't help but feel excited. He liked the billow of the tent and the sound of the ropes creaking. He also liked the smell: earthy ground and canvas. Like camping, only fun.

The lights were tried. They changed through every colour: purple, yellow, red and finally green.

As green as the glowing bug-lights when Zita was home.

Alfie had almost forgotten about the crazy stuff up at the house.

Tom Fagan came in to tighten scaffolding and check the equipment of the circus workers who were to climb to the ceiling to attach the trapezes and the high wire.

'Have a swing, Calypso?' he called out. 'Test the kit for us.'

And here was Calypso, kicking off her trainers and walking out onto the mat at the centre of the ring.

Alfie ducked behind the stands. He felt ashamed: he knew he had been rude to her.

Calypso stood very upright with one foot pointed. She reached up and grabbed a trapeze swing: a glittery bar hung on fine ropes.

She pulled herself up and swung a circle – just like a gymnast on the television!

Alfie was astonished.

He could never do that in a million years!

He stared at Calypso in admiration.

With a jump and a twist, Calypso landed on her feet with her arms raised.

Alfie forgot about hiding and stood up, clapping.

Calypso picked up her trainers and ran past him.

Alfie sat alone in the corner of the big top. The workers were taking a break, so it was a peaceful place to sit.

He was in no rush to walk back to Switherbroom Hall.

If he could even get back across the field without kissing any horses.

He took out *Everyday Magic for Beginners* and began to read.

'Have you seen a little kid?'

Alfie looked up.

'Well, have you?' It was Calypso, her face worried. 'My sister is missing. She's not quite three, green dress, red hair.'

'I haven't seen her,' said Alfie.

Calypso turned away.

'Wait, I'll help you look,' called Alfie.

Calypso nodded. 'Thank you.'

They ran around the site calling, 'NOVA! NOVA!'

'She usually stays close to our bus,' said Calypso. 'Dad will be furious – I was supposed to be minding her.'

There was no sign of a little girl with a green dress and red hair.

Alfie had an idea. 'Where does Nova like to go best?'

'To see the horses.'

But Nova was not with the horses.

'Where else?'

'The big top,' said Calypso.

'Let's go back,' said Alfie. 'It's worth a try.'

Alfie saw Nova first.

The small girl was sitting on one of the walkways made of wire and mesh.

She was up very, very high.

He pointed. 'Is that your little sister?'

'Nova!' Calypso cried in horror. 'How did you even get up there?'

Nova peeped down from her perch and began to cry.

Calypso ran to a nearby rope ladder. 'This goes up to

the walkway. There's another just there. Let's take one each, then we can help her down.'

At that point Alfie remembered that he hated heights and was in no way brave. He opened his mouth to tell Calypso, but she was already halfway up her ladder. There was nothing for it but to help Calypso save her sister. After all, hadn't Calypso saved *him* already today?

Alfie took hold of the rope ladder, which twisted away from him. He would rather kiss Shane Fagan's horse than climb this ladder. He took a deep breath, tried to ignore his shaking knees and began to climb. He was so slow that by the time he was halfway up, Calypso was helping her little sister down again rung by rung.

'It's OK, Alfie,' Calypso called up. 'You can come down now!'

Nova watched him climb back down with her blue eyes wide. When Alfie reached the ground, she clapped.

Alfie felt like clapping too.

'You were really good on the trapeze,' said Alfie shyly.

Calypso had gone and found oranges and crisps and a blanket. They would have a picnic in the big top – this time keeping a close eye on Nova! Although Calypso had told Alfie she still had no idea how her little sister had managed to climb up so high all by herself.

'You should see the experts.' Calypso pointed to the ceiling. 'They go right up there.'

Alfie shuddered. 'I couldn't do that. I hate being up high.'

'I hadn't noticed.' Calypso smiled.

Alfie reddened. 'My father made me go climbing, but it made things worse.'

Calypso thought a moment. 'Perhaps if you climbed with a friend, I could help?'

Alfie looked at Calypso in surprise. 'You'd take me up there?'

'Yes, but I'm not allowed to go right to the top.' She wrinkled her nose. 'When my mum was alive, she said it was dangerous.'

Alfie hardly knew what to say.

'She didn't fall off the trapeze or anything,' said Calypso. 'That's not what happened. I'm not really sure what happened. It was just after Nova was born. One day Mum was here and the next she wasn't. Dad said she had some kind of accident, but that's all he can tell me, although he knows much more, I'm sure of it.' She shrugged. 'The whole thing makes me angry sometimes.'

Alfie could see that Calypso was trying not to cry.

'I don't have a mum either,' he said.

Calypso glanced up at him. 'You don't?'

'Or a dad now. That's why I've come to live with my aunts.'

Thankfully Calypso didn't ask any questions. Alfie didn't want to tell the story about the lion and the sausages, or the leaky boat and the rough sea and the angry birds on the rocky island.

She might think it was all a bad joke and laugh.

'I'm sorry about earlier,' said Alfie. 'In the field, I was mean—'

'It's OK.'

They sat quietly. Listening to Nova singing to her orange. She rolled it along and then she pretended it was climbing up the leg of a bench.

Calypso laughed. 'Nova wants everything to be a squirrel.'

'Sk-weerl,' said Nova gravely.

Calypso hugged her sister. 'Yes, squirrel.'

Alfie noticed Calypso's necklace. 'What's that, on your necklace?'

Calypso took it out for Alfie to look at: a tiny white bird on a silver chain.

It looked familiar.

'It's a dove,' she said. 'Nova has one too; they were from Mum.'

Alfie thought about the Blackstacks and the Morrows – the ravens and the doves.

He suddenly wished he could tell Calypso about all the strange things that had happened to him since he arrived in the village.

Calypso wasn't exactly ordinary herself.

Would she keep a secret?

He could show her the snow globe.

But wait!

Alfie put his hand in his anorak pocket – the snow globe had gone!

'What is it, Alfie?' asked Calypso.

'I've lost something.'

Then Alfie saw it – a bright green flash under the bench. Calypso saw it too.

Nova was playing with the snow globe – she was laughing at it!

The snow globe sparked and spun.

Alfie grabbed the globe and went to stuff it in his anorak pocket.

'What is that?' cried Calypso. 'Let me see!'

Alfie hesitated, but then he held it out to her. 'Give it a moment and the blizzard will stop.'

Calypso and Nova drew nearer.

When the snow stopped swirling, Alfie saw that the scene inside the snow globe had changed. Gone was Switherbroom Hall. In its place was Mrs Mention's Tea Room. Snow frosted the window ledges and the roof and lay on the street outside. Calypso watched in astonishment as the tea-room door opened and footprints crunched down the path.

And there was the imp. Pressing his nose against the glass globe, his yellow eyes full of mischief.

Calypso's eyes widened. 'What is *that*?'

'An imp,' said Alfie.

The imp took a few steps back and pointed at the tea room and danced a jig, kicking out his spindly legs.

Nova chuckled with delight.

'What does he want?' asked Calypso.

'I think he wants us to visit Mrs Mention's Tea Room,' said Alfie. 'He probably wants to play a trick on us. Imps are nasty, tricksy creatures, apparently.'

'He can't be all that bad; Nova likes him, look!'

Nova was singing to the snow globe.

'What if he's sending us on some kind of *adventure*?' Alfie's face was worried.

'All the better!' Calypso grinned. 'Come on, Alfie. Will we go?'

What could Alfie say?

CHAPTER 7

Tea-Room Bash

Calypso lifted Nova into the pushchair, then stood and put on her disguise – a blue wig and a pair of sunglasses.

'Alfie, I'm not allowed in Mrs Mention's Tea Room.' Calypso straightened her wig. 'No circus folk, remember?'

'I think you look more obvious now.'

'But do I look like *me*?' Calypso peered over her sunglasses. She did really.

'Maybe not so much,' said Alfie kindly.

Nova cried for the snow globe.

'Hold it very tightly,' Alfie said as he put it in her hands. 'Don't drop it or it might break or roll away.'

Nova nodded very seriously and clung to the snow globe as they went into town. From time to time she kissed it and laughed at the imp inside.

*

As they neared Mrs Mention's Tea Room they could see through the window, past the flouncy pink curtains, that the place was heaving with old ladies.

'What should we do, Alfie?' asked Calypso.

'We'll go in and order tea,' Alfie frowned. 'Then maybe the imp will tell us why he's brought us here.'

'The imp can be helpful, don't forget; didn't he help you find the library?'

'He chased me there!' Alfie glanced at Calypso.

She grinned back at him.

Alfie had told Calypso everything during the walk into town. She had already seen the imp in the snow globe; why not tell her the rest? Besides, he was bursting to tell someone. About Mr Fingerhut, who seemed to know all about magic and had given him the snow globe. About Switherbroom Hall's haunted library and his aunts being witches who owned Familiars, pickled children, grew cucumber noses and slurped slug stew.

As with the imp in the snow globe, Calypso had taken it all rather well. She had listened carefully to everything Alfie had told her, nodding from time to time.

'You don't seem very . . . shocked,' he had said to her.

Calypso had thought for a moment. 'I am a bit, Alfie. But the funny thing is that what you're telling me reminds me of the stories my granny told me growing up.'

Alfie could only imagine what sort of stories fierce old Granny Fagan might come up with!

'You can't tell anyone what I've told you, Calypso,'

Alfie insisted. 'Not even your granny. Imagine if everyone found out that my aunts are witches!'

'I won't tell a soul. You have my word, Alfie Blackstack.'

★

Mrs Mention's customers were all very busy slurping tea and munching cakes, spreading gossip or rummaging in their handbags for spectacles, or hankies, or mints, or teeth, or whatever it is old ladies keep in their handbags.

Mrs Mention sailed among them in her flowery apron, setting down plates piled with tasty treats and delivering steaming teapots.

Calypso parked Nova's pushchair, lifted up her sister and followed Alfie inside. They spotted a free table and headed towards it.

'HOLD IT RIGHT THERE!'

The talking stopped.

Alfie felt every eye in the room on them.

Mrs Mention swayed over to them with her mouth pursed. 'Where do you think you lot are going?'

'Table for three, please, with a Dainty Deluxe Tea,' ventured Alfie.

Mrs Mention narrowed her eyes. 'I have no quarrel with you, Master Blackstack.' She jabbed her thumb in Calypso's direction. 'But I won't serve a *Fagan* in my tea room.'

Calypso pulled off her wig and glared at Mrs Mention. 'We have money.'

Mrs Mention scoffed. 'But you shan't be spending it on my cakes. Your circus is not welcome in our village.'

A few of the customers nodded in agreement.

One called out, 'Hear, hear.'

'I'm starting a petition.' Mrs Mention's eyes scoured the room and she raised her voice. 'That's a list that everyone puts their name on if they want the circus to leave town.'

'Ah, that's not fair!' exclaimed Calypso.

'There are plenty who don't want you here.'

Calypso looked angry. 'And there are plenty who do.'

'We'll see about that!' said Mrs Mention.

'Cake?' Nova shook the snow globe in her hand. 'Cake?'

Mrs Mention softened. 'You're not welcome on account of the mishap with the human cannonball and the fire and the goat acrobat formation team.'

'The goats ate the vicar's underpants!' piped up one old lady joyfully.

'That had nothing to do with our goats!' cried Calypso. 'It was a windy day. His underpants probably blew away – the size of his backside.'

Nova laughed. 'Backside. BIG BACKSIDE.'

Mrs Mention's cheeks reddened. 'Vile children!' She turned and gave a little curtsey. 'Sorry, Mrs Vicar.'

The other old ladies were watching, waiting. This was the best fun they'd had in years.

The vicar's wife, a sour-faced old grunion, dabbed at the corners of her mouth with a napkin and said nothing.

The snow globe hopped from Nova's hand with a fruity chuckle and landed in a bowl of soup, splattering an old lady. The old lady took up a spoon and poked crossly at it.

The snow globe spun for a second and then jumped out of the bowl. It rolled across the table, trailing soup.

'My good tablecloth!' wailed Mrs Mention.

The snow globe bounced off a plate of pink blanc-mange, up, up into the air.

The old ladies gaped open-mouthed as the snow globe dropped down – SMACK – onto another table.

Mrs Mention moved to catch it. The snow globe twitched away and skidded off between cups and saucers, sugar bowls and milk jugs.

Mrs Mention dashed after it, sending chairs and saucers and tables flying. Her customers grabbed their handbags and leapt out of the way.

The snow globe hopped into Mrs Vicar's teacup, splashing the old crow with tea.

Mrs Vicar scrambled to her feet. 'I've never been so insulted—'

The snow globe rose up into the air and hovered right in front of Mrs Vicar's nose.

Everyone watched. Everyone waited.

The snow globe let out a loud and happy fart, spun wildly in the air and dropped to the floor.

Nova gave a squeal of delight.

'We have to catch it. It's destroying everything!' said Alfie. 'Where's it gone?'

'Over there,' Calypso pointed.

The snow globe zigzagged across the room and disappeared through the swing doors into the kitchen, leaving a puff of green smoke in its wake.

The smoke spread through the room with the ferocious smell of a thousand cabbagey blow-offs.

The customers coughed and spluttered and held table-cloths to their noses.

No one noticed the children slipping through the swing doors.

Alfie raced after the snow globe. Calypso followed, pulling Nova by the hand. The snow globe slid across Mrs Mention's kitchen floor, past the table with bowls of cake mixture about to be baked.

The snow globe spun up the wall and along the mantel-piece, knocking off ornaments until it came to a photograph in a silver frame.

Then the snow globe stopped.

'The imp wants us to look at this picture,' said Calypso. 'It's something framed from a newspaper.'

MRS MENTION WINS BATTLE TO CUT DOWN TREE!

There was a picture of Mrs Mention in front of a tree; she was holding an axe. Next to her was a smiling lady with fair hair and a white dress who looked like a celebrity.

Alfie read on:

Mrs Florence Mention, tea-room owner and local resident, has won her fight to cut down the oldest and biggest tree in Little Snoddington forest. But Mrs Mention says she has only just begun and is campaigning to have the forest cleared to build the world's biggest cake factory. She told our reporter: 'There are too many trees and not enough factories round here. And besides, that old tree was creepy.' An official agreed. 'We cut down the tree because local residents were too scared to walk past it. There had been several cases of tree roots tripping villagers up. Spooky faces had also been seen on its trunk. We had no idea that Mrs Mention was planning to build a factory.' The owner of the famous tea room says she will never give up on her dream. 'One tree down – a few hundred to go!' she trilled. 'These do-gooders think trees are more important than gorgeous cakes and pastries. That's just rot.' Local chemist Zita Blackstack, who campaigned to save the tree, said she was 'gutted'. She fumed: 'That tree was home to owls, bugs, squirrels and creatures I can't even name. Destroyed thanks to a few silly villagers making up nonsense.'

'Squirrels,' said Nova sadly.

Calypso looked dismayed. 'That poor old tree. I'm glad Mrs Mention didn't get her wish to clear the forest – the trees are still there and there's no cake factory!'

'Look!' said Alfie. 'The imp is showing us something.'

The snowstorm in the globe cleared to show a big leafy tree with a small green door at the bottom of the trunk. Above the door a sign read:

HOME SWET HOME

'Oh, Alfie – Mrs Mention cut down the imp's home – that's what he's trying to spell out to us,' said Calypso.

'ALFRED BLACKSTACK!' boomed a voice from the kitchen door. 'WHAT IS GOING ON HERE?'

CHAPTER 8

Super Nova

'Out there—' Zita pointed at the door '—is a tea room in ruins, thirty frightened villagers and one very angry Mrs Mention: EXPLAIN.'

Alfie slowly removed his hand from his anorak pocket where he had stuffed the snow globe.

'Well?' demanded Zita.

She seemed to have grown taller, thinner and fiercer. Her bat was circling the kitchen with slow flaps of his leathery wings. She whistled and he came swooping to hang upside down from her wrist.

'I always thought that was an umbrella she carried!' whispered Calypso.

'SILENCE,' Zita shouted.

Nova began to cry.

71

Zita pointed at Nova. 'Bring that and follow me.' Then she swept out of the kitchen.

Something had gone very wrong in the tea room – apart from the smashed teacups and splattered cakes, the over-turned tables and broken plates.

Mrs Vicar sat stiff and wonky in her chair.

With a start, Alfie realised Mrs Vicar's face was a paper bag with crayoned eyes, nose and mouth. Straw peeped from her neck and the cuffs of her cardigan.

Some of the customers had pumpkin heads.

'They're scarecrows!' Calypso cried out.

Nova stopped crying and widened her eyes. 'DARE CROW.'

'It'll wear off,' Zita snarled.

'Did you do this?' Alfie asked in horror.

'They were running about squawking and shouting,' said Zita. 'I couldn't hear myself think.'

'You can't just turn people into scarecrows!' exclaimed Calypso.

'Why not?'

'It's not right! How would you like it?'

Alfie nudged Calypso. 'Shh! Look at her face.'

Zita's face was changing, reddening. Her nose was growing more cucumber-like. Her black eyes flashed.

Calypso bit her lip. 'Well, it isn't right!'

'Do you want to join them?' Zita growled at Calypso. 'A turnip for a head, perhaps?'

Nova began to cry.

'And I'll turn that small one into something quiet! Like a—' Zita stopped and peered closely at the little girl. 'It has green eyes.'

'No,' said Calypso. '*Her* eyes are blue!'

But they weren't. Nova's eyes were green – a very, very bright green!

'What is happening to my sister?' wailed Calypso.

★

Nova sat on a high stool, screaming.

The stool was in Blackstacks' Chemist's Shop, in Zita's mixing room.

'Stop that noise,' said Zita, pointing at Nova.

Nova screamed on.

Calypso tried to cuddle her, but Nova just cried more.

Zita waved her hand. A bandage appeared over Nova's mouth; her eyes widened in surprise.

'Take that off!' Calypso demanded. 'You're frightening her!'

Zita reached into a jar on the shelf. She pulled out a lollipop in the shape of a skull and waved it at the little girl.

'I'll give you this,' she said, 'if you stop shouting, yes?'

The bandage over Nova's mouth disappeared. Nova blinked, gave Zita a watery smile and reached out her hand for the lollipop.

Zita then proceeded to do something very strange indeed.

First, she tapped Nova on the head with a twig, then with a feather and then with something that looked like a wizened orange on a string.

'Just as I thought,' Zita murmured to herself.

'Has this got anything to do with magic?' said Calypso.

Zita scowled. 'What gave you that idea, Calypso? There's no such thing as magic.'

'You've just turned Mrs Vicar into a scarecrow! What was that then?'

'Your imagination!'

'Her body was made of straw!' cried Calypso.

'Rot!' replied Zita.

'She had a paper bag for a head!' continued Calypso.

'Hogwash!' snorted Zita. Her nose began to swell and her face turned a startling red.

Nova pointed her lollipop at Zita and chuckled. 'Funny lady!'

Zita looked baffled. Perhaps no one had found her funny before.

Zita had been pacing backwards and forwards for the longest time, biting her long black plait in a bad-tempered way.

Now and again she stopped to stare at Nova.

And Nova smiled back.

Alfie looked around himself. He had a feeling that nothing was quite what it seemed in Zita's mixing room.

It was a curious place. Shelves were stacked with jars containing weird dried stuff and colourful powders. Occasionally a jar twitched or shuffled.

The door opened and Rafferty padded into the room; Gertrude followed, her face stern with worry.

'Mrs Mention is furious,' she said. 'Her tea room is a mess! Her customers are complaining – they don't understand why they are covered in straw!'

'Pumpkin heads,' said Zita nastily. 'The scarecrow spell's worn off then?'

'It's against the Head Witch's rules!' exclaimed Gertrude. 'Rule Number One: no turning of people non-magical or magical into objects various.'

'It was only for a few minutes! Besides, if the Head Witch breaks the rules, why shouldn't I? She's turned most of her own family into pebbles.'

Gertrude looked frightened. 'Zita, don't say such things! You'll get us into trouble. The Head Witch's spies are everywhere!'

'I'm not scared!' sneered Zita.

But Alfie noticed Zita glance around the room. So, his aunt wasn't the Head Witch then – and how scary must the Head Witch be if *Zita* was scared of her?

Gertrude turned to Calypso. 'Mrs Mention has told all her customers not to visit the circus; if they go to your show, she says she won't serve them tea and cake.'

'That's so *unfair*!' cried Calypso. 'Mrs Mention hates us because we live differently to her. She blames everything on the circus!'

'Tell us what happened,' Gertrude said kindly. 'We can help.'

There was silence, except for the sound of Nova slurping her lollipop. Alfie had no idea what to say.

'Stink bombs . . .' said Calypso. 'That's what happened.'

Alfie turned to Calypso in confusion. '*Stink bombs?*'

Calypso nodded. 'Yep.'

She looked at Alfie's anorak pocket. She was helping him keep the snow globe secret!

Surely it had caused them enough trouble, thought Alfie. *Should they just hand it over and explain to his aunts what had really happened?*

'All that mess was caused by stink bombs?' said Zita frostily. '*Really?*'

'Extra powerful!' Calypso added.

Zita turned to Alfie. 'Is this true?'

'Oh yes,' he agreed hesitantly. 'Terrible smell.'

Zita looked like she didn't believe a word of it. 'So, where did you get these stink bombs?'

'Mr Fingerhut?' suggested Alfie.

'We really must do something about Mr Fingerhut,' said Gertrude. 'The things he sells in his shop ought to come with a warning.'

'So, the three of you went into Mrs Mention's Tea Room to let off stink bombs?' puzzled Zita. 'Why would you do that?'

'For fun,' said Calypso.

'Mrs Mention didn't think it was fun,' pointed out Gertrude.

'I mean . . . we let the stink bombs off *by accident*,' said Calypso. 'We didn't *plan* to cause trouble.'

'What were you doing in Mrs Mention's kitchen?' asked Zita.

'Wrong turn,' said Calypso. 'We ran from the stink and went the wrong way.'

Magnus made a scoffing noise. He had flapped over to the hat-stand in the corner and was dangling from it like a leathery fruit.

'If you children are *lying*, there will be consequences,' glowered Zita. '*Dreadful* consequences.'

From the ferocious look on Zita's face Alfie did not doubt this.

He wondered what life would be like as a scarecrow.

He had the clothes for it.

Gertrude looked at the shrivelled orange, the feather and the twig on the workbench. 'You tested someone, Zita?'

'That small noisy one.'

'You *tested* Nova?' Calypso asked. 'What for?'

'Nothing,' muttered Zita.

'She's my sister – tell me! I already know you're witches!' Calypso blurted.

'Zita was testing Nova to see if she's also a witch,' said Gertrude.

Everyone turned and looked at Nova. She had crept into the wastepaper basket with Rafferty and was fast asleep, snuggled into his warm belly.

Nova squeezed Rafferty's tail in her sleep. The cat purred.

'She's only little!' exclaimed Calypso. 'How could she be a witch?'

'Sometimes witches are born . . . *witchy*,' replied Gertrude. 'Everyone else has to learn how to be one.'

Calypso seemed cheered by this idea. 'So, I could learn how to be a witch and then turn Mrs Mention into a scarecrow?'

Zita laughed.

'No, Calypso, you couldn't.' Gertrude's voice was strict. 'Because that sort of thing is forbidden.'

Calypso looked disappointed. 'I would have loved to have seen Mrs Mention with a pumpkin head! Wouldn't you, Alfie?'

Alfie nodded. But there had been no sign of Mrs Mention among the other scarecrows as they were leaving the tea room.

'Anyway, what makes you think Nova is a witch?' asked Calypso. 'She doesn't know any spells.'

'Her eyes turned green,' Zita answered. 'But anyway, she has no magic.'

'Are you sure?' said Gertrude.

'Of course!' snapped Zita.

But Alfie thought that Zita didn't look at all sure.

Calypso pushed Nova's pushchair in silence. The little girl was awake now, singing and waving what was left of her lollipop at the sky.

'Imagine them thinking Nova was a witch!' said Calypso.

78

Nova, her eyes still a bit greenish, beamed a smile. She was the only one of them who looked happy.

Alfie took the snow globe from his pocket. It was sticky and smeary with soup and blancmange.

'Maybe we should have shown this to my aunts? We could still? Imps cause trouble, that's what the ghost librarian at Switherbroom Hall said.'

Calypso shook her head. 'It's too late now. We'd have to admit we lied about the stink bomb. Can you imagine how angry your Aunt Zita would be?'

Alfie thought of Zita's terrifying red face, her cucumber nose and the juicy warts.

'We'll just have to make sure the imp doesn't cause any more trouble,' added Calypso. 'Anyhow, let's get this job over with.'

They had a letter to deliver.

Gertrude had made them write an apology. It said:

Dear Mrs Mention,
 We are SORRY for causing MAYHEM in your tea room. We didn't mean to. We will not do it again.
 We apologise from the bottom of our hearts!
 Yours truly,
 Alfie, Calypso and Nova

At the bottom Nova had drawn a squirrel jumping from a cake and the snow globe hitting Mrs Vicar in the eye.

Thankfully only Nova could tell what the drawing was of.

When they arrived at Mrs Mention's Tea Room, the door was locked and the curtains drawn.

A sign said:

CLOSED
Due to DAMAGE caused by
Fagan's Family Circus
DOWN WITH THE CIRCUS!
FAGANS LEAVE TOWN!

Calypso's face reddened. 'Oh, she's a horror!'

She snatched the letter from Alfie and squashed it through the letterbox.

They walked on in silence.

The snow globe buzzed in Alfie's pocket. He groaned, 'More mischief.'

He took it out and waited. The blizzard cleared to reveal Mr Fingerhut's Fun Emporium.

Calypso thought a moment. 'That's not a bad idea, Alfie. We might be able to find out more about the snow globe.'

'Or give it back to Mr Fingerhut – I'm sure this imp will lead us into trouble again if we're not careful!'

CHAPTER 9

A Visitor to Switherbroom Hall

Mr Fingerhut's shop was also closed. Like Mrs Mention he had put a sign up. His sign read:

Gone Fishing

Alfie looked through the window at the jumble of clutter inside. There was no sign of Mr Fingerhut or of the stuffed weasel behind his counter.

'What'll we do now?' asked Calypso.

'Wait a while?'

They parked Nova's pushchair and sat down on the curb. The road was quiet and the day still warm.

Nova seemed happy enough playing with her chewed-up lollipop stick. She made it squeak, then hid it under her leg. Then she pulled it back out again.

'Imp,' said Nova. 'IMP. IMP.'

Calypso glanced at Alfie. 'There's something else unusual about Nova, apart from her eyes turning green.'

'Oh?'

'How did she get up so high in the big top, Alfie?'

'I don't know.'

Calypso looked at Alfie. 'I can't quite believe magic is real. But then again, I can.'

'I know what you mean,' agreed Alfie. 'It's sort of weird and oddly normal all at once.'

Calypso thought a moment. 'Have you ever wanted wonderful, dangerous, magical things to happen to you?'

Alfie shook his head. 'No, never.'

'You've never really wished for an adventure?'

'I don't like adventures,' replied Alfie.

'But we're having one, aren't we?' Calypso sighed. 'I only wish I knew more about magic!'

'You could read the book I found in the library; it's all in there.'

'Oh, books don't know everything, Alfie!'

A raven flapped down from the roof of Mr Fingerhut's shop. It landed on the handle of Nova's pushchair.

The raven held an envelope in its beak.

Nova laughed and offered the bird her lollipop stick.

The raven dropped the envelope, gave a caw and flew away.

Alfie picked up the envelope. It was addressed to him.

Master Alfred Blackstack

Alfie had never received a letter before. Let alone one delivered by a raven!

'It's for me!' he exclaimed.

'Open it!' urged Calypso.

Alfie opened the envelope carefully. Inside was a note, green ink on black paper.

Alfred,
  A TIP.
  May be USEFUL on your ADVENTURE.
  When in doubt, visit a LIBRARY (like the one at Switherbroom Hall, for example).
  Yours, etc.,
  Ignatius Fingerhut
  P.S. Yes, Calypso, books do *know everything.*
  *P.P.S. Don't believe what they say about imps –
imps are really rather nice.*

Calypso looked around. 'Mr Fingerhut heard me talking! But where is he?' Her eyes were wide.

'I've no idea.' Alfie pointed down the street; a van had turned the corner and was driving towards them. 'But isn't that your dad?'

Calypso groaned.

Tom Fagan pulled his van over to the side of the road. 'Alfie, Cal. Pop Nova in the seat there; I'll bring her home for her nap. And try to stay out of any more trouble.'

Calypso grimaced. 'You've heard?'

'I had Mrs Mention up at the camp just now; she wasn't in a good mood.'

'The mean thing! You know she's never liked us being here, Dad!'

'We may have to leave town.'

'Because of today?' asked Calypso, horrified. 'We didn't mean to cause trouble and we've apologised in a letter.'

'She has the village on her side now,' said Tom.

'Oh, the nasty—'

'That's enough, Cal.' Tom's voice was stern. 'Promise me, both of you, not to do anything to make matters worse.'

Alfie and Calypso nodded glumly.

They walked back through the forest in silence, Alfie feeling brave enough to take the short cut with Calypso beside him.

He glanced at her. 'I'm sorry. I had no idea the snow globe would get you into trouble.'

'It's not your fault, Alfie.'

They reached Switherbroom Hall. There was a big shiny white car parked outside. The driver, in a white hat and uniform, stood waiting.

'Who's that?' asked Calypso.

'No idea,' answered Alfie. 'There's a flag on the front of the car, which usually means it belongs to someone important.'

The front door of Switherbroom Hall opened. Out came a stranger dressed in black, followed by Zita.

'Quick, hide.' Alfie pulled Calypso back into the forest, ducking behind a fallen tree log.

'Why?'

'That visitor!' said Alfie. 'She gives me the creeps even more than Zita does.'

Calypso peeped over the log. 'I see what you mean.'

The stranger seemed to be wearing a rucksack under her black cloak, for there was a bulge at her back. Her legs, in black tights, were as skinny as sticks. She had a long, sharp-featured face and her head was set into her shoulders, with no neck to be seen. She wore a headband pulled low.

The stranger started to move down the steps.

Calypso made a face. 'Ugh! She has such an odd way of moving. She scuttles.'

'Like a spider,' shuddered Alfie.

The driver opened the car door and Zita climbed in. The strange scuttling person climbed in after her.

'Zita's leaving with her,' whispered Alfie.

As the car drove away, it passed the hiding children. They ducked. Alfie caught sight of the flag. It was a picture of a white dove – the exact same dove as on Calypso's necklace.

The sign of the great magical Morrow family!

Alfie had a thought. He turned to Calypso. 'Your last name is Fagan, isn't it?'

Calypso hesitated. 'Yes.'

Alfie had another thought. 'Has your last name always been Fagan?'

'More or less.' Calypso looked away.

'Have you ever heard the name Morrow?' said Alfie.

Calypso blushed.

'Calypso?'

'I have to go. It's nearly dinner time.'

'What about Mr Fingerhut's note? We were going to speak to the library ghost.'

Calypso was suddenly looking anxious. 'I don't want to get into any more trouble, Alfie.'

But she always seemed so brave! Alfie had seen her on the trapeze and standing up to his ferocious aunt. Even so, perhaps the creepy spidery stranger had alarmed Calypso?

Or had Switherbroom Hall frightened her?

It *was* spooky, nestled in the dark forest with its wonky roof and windows and green smoke twisting out of the chimneys.

Or maybe it was the idea of meeting a ghost that worried Calypso?

'It's not about the ghost, is it?' asked Alfie. 'He's really quite friendly.'

Calypso didn't answer.

Alfie realised that it was something to do with her name. She was acting oddly because there was something she needed to hide from him!

He tried again. 'Calypso, your necklace—'

Calypso stood up and brushed dirt off her knees. 'Be seeing you, Alfie.'

'Can we hang out tomorrow?' Alfie asked.

But Calypso was gone.

CHAPTER 10

Cats and Butter Dishes

Gertrude sat at the kitchen table not eating her breakfast. Her hair was blue today and she was wearing a dark green dress, not her multi-coloured leggings. But that wasn't it. Alfie realised what was different about her: Gertrude looked *serious*, really, really serious.

She frowned down at the toast she had barely nibbled. 'It's good of you to help out, Alfie.'

Gertrude had an important errand to run. She had asked Alfie to mind the shop while she was gone.

Alfie was surprised. He was only nine and knew nothing about chemist's shops.

But it was nice to be trusted.

Alfie's father had never trusted Alfie to do anything.

Mr Blackstack asked Alfie to hold his binoculars. Alfie dropped them and they smashed.

Mr Blackstack asked Alfie to fold up the tent. Alfie got tangled in the guy-lines.

'Are you sure you want me to help?' he asked his aunt. 'I don't always get things right.'

'Neither do I, Alfie – neither does anyone!'

Gertrude stirred her tea with a butter knife and spooned sugar on her toast. She stared out of the kitchen window and sighed.

'Don't worry, Aunt Gertrude,' said Alfie. 'I'll take good care of the shop.'

'Rafferty will help you.'

The cat in the corner looked up from washing his paws.

'If any customers come in, write down what they want,' said Gertrude, 'and I'll deliver their orders later.'

Alfie nodded. That sounded easy enough.

'Do you have any questions, Alfie?'

Alfie did, of course, but not about the shop.

'Yesterday there was a white car outside. It had a flag with a dove on it.'

Gertrude seemed to grow a little pale. 'Yes, we had a visitor.'

'Aunt Zita left with her.'

'She did.' Gertrude leant forward, her voice low. 'Perhaps the less we say about that, the better, Alfie.'

Alfie tried another question. 'Isn't the dove the sign of the Morrow family? I read about the Blackstacks and the Morrows in a book from the library.'

'The car belongs to Prunella Morrow, the Head Witch.'

'That was Prunella Morrow, that person all in black?'

Gertrude shook her head. 'No, that was her personal guard, Featherlegs.'

'She was so creepy.'

'She's also Prunella's Familiar.'

Alfie thought about this. 'But she's a person and the book says that only animals and birds can be Familiars.'

'That's right. Featherlegs used to be a spider.'

Alfie's eyes widened. 'She moved just like a spider – she scuttled!'

'Prunella was trying to cast a spell on an enemy. Featherlegs was in the way and now she's stuck somewhere between a witch and a spider.'

'That's awful.'

'Magic can be awful, Alfie.' Gertrude took a sip of buttery tea. 'But then most spells wear off. Let's say someone annoys you and you turn them into a plum—'

'A plum?'

'Or a mouse, or a spoon, or whatever. All well and good if the spell wears off.'

'Is it?' asked Alfie. 'I'm not sure I'd like to be any of those things.'

'Just watch.' Gertrude took a silver bottle from the shelf above the cooker and sprinkled green powder onto the palm of her hand. 'Do you mind, Raffy?'

The cat jumped up onto the table.

Gertrude blew the powder over Rafferty, closed her eyes and muttered a few words.

And there, in place of the cat, was a fat orange teapot.

Rafferty changed back with a puff of green smoke and spat on the tablecloth.

'Oh, I forgot. Rafferty hates the taste of tea. Next time I'll make you a butter dish, dear!'

The cat purred.

'Can I try?' Alfie asked, surprising both himself and his aunt.

Gertrude hesitated.

Alfie waited for his aunt to say no.

'All right,' said Gertrude.

The cat flinched.

Rafferty sat very still on the table. Gertrude sprinkled green powder into Alfie's hand. It sparkled like Christmas glitter and stuck in places; Alfie's palm was sweaty because he was nervous.

The cat looked nervous too.

Alfie had to learn the spell, but it rhymed (as spells have to, of course), which made it easier to remember.

This was the spell:

Cat plump and nimble with marmalade fur,
Tummy tickles make you purr.
Hang on to your whiskers – here's my wish:
For five seconds you'll be a butter dish.

Gertrude explained that you don't need to use fancy words in a magic spell, but you do need to use the right words. For example, if you said 'turnip' instead of 'butter dish', you'd have a vegetable. If you said 'a week' instead of five seconds, then, oh dear . . .

'The most important thing, Alfie,' she added, 'is to imagine the spell *will work*; close your eyes if you need to.'

'Righto, imagining the spell.' Alfie closed his eyes.

'You might want to open your eyes while you blow the powder over the cat.'

Alfie opened his eyes.

'Off you go, Alfie,' Gertrude encouraged. 'And don't be disappointed if nothing happens. It might not work the first time.'

Alfie nodded, blew the powder, shut his eyes and said the spell.

He imagined Rafferty changing shape.

Then he opened his eyes again.

There was no cat.

Instead there was a butter dish in the middle of the table. The very one he'd imagined – orange and white and flowery!

'You're a natural!' whooped Gertrude.

'Crikey,' said Alfie.

The butter dish flickered and turned back into a fat ginger cat.

The cat sneezed.

'I'm glad you're a cat again!' said Alfie. 'And not a butter dish for ever!'

Gertrude nodded. 'But then a Forever Spell is against the law, of course, unless you're the Head Witch.'

'That doesn't sound fair.'

'It's not,' said Gertrude quietly. 'It's very easy to get into trouble with the Head Witch and you'd find yourself turned into something much worse than a butter dish.'

Alfie thought again about the white car taking his aunt away. 'Is Zita in trouble with the Head Witch?'

Gertrude pursed her lips. 'Zita has been accused of writing rude things about our leader in the *Daily Witch* newspaper.'

'What sort of things?'

'That we should get rid of the Head Witch,' whispered Gertrude. 'Because she's wicked.'

How terrifying must the Head Witch be, Alfie thought, *if Zita thinks she's wicked?*

'The Head Witch makes up rules for everyone else to follow,' continued Gertrude, 'while she does whatever she wants. If anyone disagrees with her, then she turns them into something frightful or sends them to prison. She has even made her own family disappear – the ones that might try to replace her!'

'Can't you get a new Head Witch?'

'Not without a Witch War.'

'A Witch War?'

'Witch Wars happen when a Head Witch goes properly rotten.'

Alfie couldn't help thinking of the scarecrows in the tea room with their pumpkin faces gone all soft and mouldy. It was a horrible thought.

'Can you imagine the worst possible playground bully?' said Gertrude.

Alfie nodded. He'd met a few of those.

'Now give that bully tremendous powers – the power to change your whole family into snails or specks of sand and there's nothing you can do about it.'

'Have many Head Witches gone rotten?' asked Alfie.

'A few, but Prunella has *always* been rotten, even as a girl, long before she was Head Witch.'

'You knew her then?'

Gertrude nodded. 'And she's always had a special hatred for us Blackstacks.'

'What happens in a Witch War?' asked Alfie.

'Witches take sides and old quarrels are remembered. The Blackstacks and the Morrows have always been enemies and the other witch families follow. In the last Witch War, when I was small, thousands were lost. Forever Spells were used and those poor witches could not be saved.' Gertrude shuddered. 'Our own Granny Blackstack was turned into a stick; she's on the mantelpiece in the parlour.'

'That's awful. I can't imagine what being a stick would be like.'

'Neither can I,' said Gertrude.

They sat together quietly for a while, lost in their own thoughts. Until Alfie tried another question. 'Where has the Head Witch taken Zita?'

'I don't know, Alfie.'

Gertrude got up from the table and went to the cooker.

'I have to try to talk to Prunella,' she said miserably, poking at something in a pot. 'There's no other way to help my sister. If Zita has been put in prison, it will be impossible to find her, let alone get her out.'

Alfie thought about what he knew about prisons. 'Aren't prisons quite easy to spot, with high walls and bars on the windows?'

Gertrude put the lid back on the pot and sat down again, her face suddenly gloomy. 'Witches have a different sort of prison, Alfie. The witches are shrunk and put in glass jars. Then these "witch bottles" are hidden in secret places. Zita could be anywhere.'

Alfie thought about the imp; he was imprisoned too, but at least he could change the scene in the snow globe.

'Imagine how furious Zita will be!' Alfie exclaimed. 'Trapped in a jar, like a tadpole!'

Gertrude frowned. 'This is serious matter, Alfie. Unless the Head Witch releases her, I might not see my sister again.'

★

Alfie and Rafferty walked to Blackstacks' Chemist's Shop. Alfie with the snow globe zipped into his anorak pocket and Rafferty showing every sign of being a marmalade cat and not a butter dish.

Alfie opened the shutters and unlocked the door, and Rafferty climbed into the shop window ready for his morning snooze.

Alfie checked the till. There were notes and coins ready

in their compartments. He neatened the pile of paper bags behind the counter. Each had the name BLACKSTACKS' stamped on it and a picture of a raven. He glanced up at the shelves. The packages and bottles, tubes and jars were well behaved today. There were a few shuffles and scuffles when he turned the key in the door, but mostly they had stayed quite still.

A row of tubs stood side by side along the lower shelves. Alfie read the labels:

BUM CREAM, FACE CREAM, WART CREAM,
CUSTARD CREAM

On the shelves above, packets were stacked neatly:

STOMACH POWDER, HEADACHE POWDER,
FART POWDER

Above them, a row of tins, each labelled with a small sticker:

NOSTRIL UNBLOCKERS, SPLINTER TEASERS,
THUMB HATS

On the very top shelf, the jars were black with red skulls on:

RAT POISON, ANT POISON, POSTMAN
POISON

95

The door to Zita's mixing room was closed. The sign on it said:

PRIVATE – NO ENTRY

Alfie tried the door handle and peeped inside.

The room was empty. No fierce aunt or nasty flapping bat.

He could take a peek – what would be the harm?

First, Alfie looked at the weird dried things in jars. Then he looked at the weird dried things in the drawers. Then he looked at the weird old books on the bookcase.

One of them stood out: a huge book with a black velvet cover.

Alfie took it to the workbench, staggering under its weight. He opened it carefully.

The front page had Zita's name written on it.

ZITALINA HORTENSIA AQUILEGIA BLACKSTACK

Neat handwriting in green ink covered page after page. There were recipes for Nit Baths and Hiccup Cures, Teeth Tonics and De-Wrinkling Creams. Some of the ingredients were strange to say the least:

One back-door key, well rusted
A pinch of powdered swan foot
One fresh tongue (any kind), finely chopped

One recipe drew Alfie's attention. It was scribbled down next to a cure for ear maggots:

BLACKSTACKS' GENTLE FRIENDLINESS TONIC
Promotes understanding and kindliness.
Dose: Two tablespoonsful twice a day.
Three tablespoons three times a day if the patient is extremely bad-tempered.
(If mixed on a Wednesday, you will have a cure for weevil infestation.)

Zita should make some of this Gentle Friendliness Tonic for herself. Or perhaps Alfie could make a batch and pop it in her slug stew.

Then Alfie felt guilty: after all, Zita could be in some terrible witch prison.

He'd be better off tipping this tonic into Mrs Mention's teapots. That would sort those mean villagers! They would all buy a ticket for the show and the circus would stay and so would Calypso.

Alfie found paper and a pencil and took note of the recipe.

He read on until he found another interesting spell:

GREAT AUNT MURGATROYD'S NO-RISK FLOATING CORDIAL
A LIFESAVER for Rock Climbers, Helicopter Pilots and Trampoline Artists

Alfie copied down the recipe. If he ever had to climb on anything higher than a chair again – not that he planned to – this was one magical remedy he'd want to have to hand.

Alfie folded the copied-out spells carefully and unzipped the pocket of his anorak.

That was funny . . .

There was a big hole in his pocket – the snow globe had gone!

There'd been no hole in his pocket when he'd put the snow globe into it. Alfie searched the shop; the snow globe was nowhere to be found. He would have to retrace his steps to Switherbroom Hall.

At that moment the shop bell jingled and his first customer arrived.

Alfie forgot all about the snow globe.

Calypso's face was deathly pale. 'Alfie, something dreadful has happened. It's Nova – she's disappeared!'

CHAPTER 11

Nova Vanishes!

Alfie and Calypso threaded through vans and tents. Calypso's bus was set apart, further into the trees.

Inside, the bus was bright and tidy, with painted cupboards, a table and built-in seats. At the end of the bus there were bunk beds with a curtain for a door.

'That's where I last saw Nova,' explained Calypso. 'She was on her bed playing with her toys, there was a green flash and—'

'There was a green flash?'

'Yes, just like when she was playing with the snow globe in the big top.' She paused. 'That's why I came to you for help, Alfie, and not the grown-ups.' She lowers her voice. 'Magic happens with a green flash, doesn't it?'

Alfie looked around. 'But could Nova have got out?'

99

Calypso shook her head. 'The window above our bunks is too high. And I was sitting on the steps, so she didn't get out that way.'

They sat down at the table. Alfie felt glad of the open windows, for the day was already heating up. It was a day for eating ice creams and swimming – not running around after vanished little sisters!

'The snow globe!' remembered Alfie. He showed Calypso the hole in his pocket. 'It's escaped.'

'Do you think it had something to do with Nova disappearing? The green flash?'

'Well, they're both missing, aren't they?'

'Alfie, there's something I need to tell you.' Calypso's face was very serious.

'Go on.'

'My mum's name was Ursula Morrow.' Calypso bit her lip. 'I'm sorry I didn't tell you yesterday. Especially after you told me your secrets about magic!'

'It's OK,' said Alfie. 'I did wonder when I saw the dove on your necklace.'

Calypso nodded. 'It's just that Mum made me promise never to tell anyone; she told me that I was to *always* use the name Fagan.'

Alfie smiled at her. 'Really, it's OK.'

'Mum never told me about magic and now all this weird stuff's going on: Nova's eyes changing colour, finding her up so high in the big top.' Calypso hesitated. 'Do you think these things are happening because we are Morrows?'

'I don't know, Calypso,' said Alfie. 'Let's just search the bus and see if there are any clues.'

Alfie and Calypso emptied drawers, tumbling out their contents. They pulled clothes and toys out of cupboards and boxes. They even searched in the old bell tent outside, where Granny Fagan stayed because she liked to smoke her pipe.

They would have to tell Tom Fagan and perhaps even the police that Nova was missing. The camp would have to be searched. How would they explain about the green flash, or the snow globe, or the fact that magic and witches and imps were real?

Calypso went inside the bus to get them some juice, for the day was very hot now. Alfie heard her shout. He ran into the bus.

There, on the table, was the snow globe.

'It wasn't there before, Alfie!'

'I know – we searched the whole bus!'

Alfie and Calypso peered into the snow globe. The snow blizzard was clearing. They saw a tiny version of Calypso's bus, the very bus they were in! Only the snow globe's bus had red letters painted on its side spelling the word:

INCOMIN

'The imp is sending us a message!' exclaimed Alfie.

On the side of the snow globe's bus, new words appeared. They said:

I HAV YOR BABBY

The red letters shuffled about, then more appeared, making a new sentence:

LET ME OUT OR I KEEP YOR BABBY

'That's kidnapping!' Calypso grabbed the snow globe. 'Give my sister back, imp!'

Nothing happened.

Then Calypso gave a howl of anger. She showed the snow globe to Alfie.

YOU HERD

'Why would the imp even take her? She's only a little girl?' raged Calypso.

The letters on the bus rearranged themselves:

LET ME OUT AN I GVE HER BAK

'All right, imp,' said Alfie. 'How do we let you out?'

Inside the snow globe, the letters formed the word:

KEY

At the base of the snow globe a keyhole appeared, flashing green.

'OK, a key,' noted Calypso. 'Where do we find this key?'

The words rewrote themselves:

HED WITC

'*Head Witch*. Are you saying that *Prunella Morrow* has the key?' asked Alfie.

There was a pause. Then:

YEP – PINCH IT OFF HER

'So, all we have to do,' said Calypso, in a voice that was brighter than her face looked. 'Is find this Head Witch and pinch the key—'

'Pinch something? From the Head Witch?' said Alfie. 'But she's terrible!'

'She can't be that terrible if she's a Morrow,' said Calypso with a bitter smile. 'I'm probably related to her.'

'Don't joke about that, Calypso. There was a reason your mum told you never to use that name.'

'What reason, Alfie?'

'Prunella Morrow is really bad, for one!'

Calypso frowned. 'How bad?'

'She turns people into pebbles! She's put Zita in prison for writing about her in a newspaper.'

The letters scrambled and shuffled. Then:

INVIT HER TO TEA

Calypso nodded grimly. 'All right. I want my sister back. If I have to invite some terrible Head Witch or other to tea, I'll do it.'

Alfie said nothing. He had a bad feeling about this.

'In the meantime, you'd better not hurt my sister, imp!' Calypso told the snow globe.

Then she let out a cry of surprise. 'Look, Alfie!'

Inside the snow globe, sitting on the steps of the tiny bus, was Nova. She was wearing a green hat with a feather in it.

'Nova!' Calypso called. 'Nova!'

The tiny Nova inside the snow globe waved and smiled.

The imp pressed its nose to the other side of the glass. Their view of Nova was lost.

'We'll get the key,' Alfie said to the imp sternly. 'But you must keep Nova safe and not harm her!'

The imp blew a raspberry. They heard Nova laugh with glee.

The snowstorm swirled.

CHAPTER 12

Prunella's Diary

'He must be an actual *ghost*,' said Calypso. 'Because we can *see* him but also see *through* him!'

'Keep your voice down,' replied Alfie. 'He'll hear you.'

'A real live ghost though, Alfie!'

The ghostly librarian scowled out from under his glimmering bonnet. 'Shh!'

'Why are we even here, Alfie?' grumbled Calypso. 'What can a dusty old library tell us about rescuing my sister?'

Alfie studied the shelves of books. 'There must be some way to get Nova back without involving the Head Witch. She honestly sounds scary, Calypso.'

Calypso looked down her nose at him. 'I'm not scared of her.'

'Well, I am,' murmured Alfie. 'Look, the library helped me before. Let's just see if any interesting books pick us.'

Calypso rolled her eyes. 'Really, Alfie, I can't imagine—'

Alfie nudged her and pointed. A book was sliding itself shyly out of a row of similar books.

Alfie took the book from the shelf and showed her the title:

A Complete History of Wood Imps

Calypso groaned.

'Well, we are dealing with an imp, aren't we?' said Alfie. 'It wouldn't hurt to learn more about them . . . That's funny; there are no pages inside.'

A big square had been cut in the pages and nestled inside was—

'A secret diary!' declared Calypso. 'Hidden inside the book!'

'How do you know it's a secret diary?'

'Why else would it be locked?' said Calypso, examining the tiny padlock on the side. 'I can't see how it can be opened though: it doesn't seem to have a keyhole.'

'Maybe with a code word?' suggested Alfie. 'Chances are it's a magical diary, too, if it's in here.'

'*Open sesame!*'

'Well, probably not that,' said Alfie.

But the tiny padlock swung open. Calypso grinned and read the first line out loud:

My name is Prunella Morrow, I am ten years old and this is my diary.

Calypso turned to Alfie, her face shocked. 'This was the Head Witch's diary when she was a girl! But what's it doing here?'

The library ghost drifted over. 'I believe that book was found in the forest a long time ago. Never looked inside, not being a fan of imps, you see.'

Calypso took the diary and began to turn the pages. 'She had such neat writing. Prunella was not much older than us when she wrote this. Oh Alfie, listen.'

She read aloud:

EVERYONE has got it WRONG! They think Ursula is the good one just because she is popular and always smiling! My annoying little sister has friends to spare but I sit alone in the playground every day.

   Don't they know I'm going to be Head Witch when I grow up?! (Dear Diary – YOU know my greatest dream!)

'NO WAY!' cried Calypso. 'That means the Head Witch is my—'

'Aunt,' said the library ghost, nodding sadly. For once he didn't have the heart to 'shh'!

Calypso read on.

Even Mama and Papa like Ursula better than me, and I spend hours trudging through the forest helping Papa with his work! How I hate visiting

Little Snoddington: the gloomy drippy forest and the village all riddled with Blackstacks! But it's where the best wood imps are to be found. Papa wastes his time with these creatures and they play pranks on him! They knot his beard and steal his hat and turn the ink in his pen into gravy. How I'd love to cut down their trees and send them all running. Maybe that's why he likes Ursula best – she's just like those annoying creatures. She doesn't do a thing to help him and yet Papa laughs at all her silly circus stunts – the ones she's been learning from those loathsome Fagans all summer. I can't remember ever making Papa laugh.

'I almost feel sorry for her,' said Calypso.

Alfie nodded. He knew what it was like to sit alone in a playground day after day.

Calypso turned the pages quickly, stopping to read another page aloud:

I knew it! Ursula has not been going to learn circus skills with the Fagans at all! My wonderful sister has been sneaking off to play with PHINEAS BLACKSTACK – A BLACKSTACK!

She says they are best friends and BEGGED me not to tell on them.

'Phineas Blackstack was my father,' said Alfie.

Calypso looked up from the diary. 'So, *my* mother and *your* father were best friends? Just like us!'

Alfie nodded. He was too happy to speak. He'd never had a friend, let alone a *best* friend.

Calypso continued reading:

EVERYTHING has gone wrong! Of course I told on Ursula and she has been banned from seeing her Blackstack friend FOR EVER! But I'm no more popular than before! Mama and Papa seem to like me less and Ursula has told everyone I'm a tell-tale.

Calypso turned page after page, engrossed.

'What happened next?' Alfie asked.

'Prunella caused more trouble!' said Calypso, and read:

Phineas Blackstack came up to me in the village today. I refused to talk to him, so he chased me down an alleyway (the beast!). He told me that he is being sent back to school early – there will be no more summer holidays for him. As if I care! He told me I was cruel to tell on him and Ursula.

I told him I wasn't the only one to tell – that his darling sisters Zita and Gertrude (PAH! PAH!) were quite the tattletales! This is quite true, because Papa said that the Blackstack girls had been questioned and told their parents everything! They'd known about Ursula and Phineas for ages, of course, the toerags.

Beastly Blackstack told me he no longer cares for Little Snoddington, or his sisters, or magic. He is off to study birds – they are far less trouble.

It makes me happy to think of the Blackstack children all miserable and quarrelling – aren't they our enemies?!

As for my sister, she says she hates me entirely and when she's grown up she'll find Phineas and they'll both run away with the circus!!! Ursula says I'll make a great Head Witch because then I can order people to like me, which is the only way they will. Ursula has to come to the forest every day now to help Papa, having forfeited her circus training (HA!). I have to hide in a tree trunk to write this away from her nosy beak.

'Prunella must have lost this diary when she was writing it secretly in the forest,' said Calypso. 'Oh, Alfie, hear this bit.'

Diary dearest here is my promise:

When I am Head Witch (if old Dame Riddle Blackstack ever falls off her perch), I'll find a way to reverse the Forever Spell. I'll change Granny Morrow from a chair to a witch again and together we will RULE OVER EVERYONE as the most powerful witches in the universe.

Oh, and I'll turn Ursula into a pebble and throw her into the sea.

Calypso turned to Alfie. 'My mum never mentioned having a sister, not once. They must have stayed enemies. Mum ran away with the circus and Prunella got her wish and became the Head Witch.'

'I didn't know about my aunts either – and Prunella was the reason why my father fell out with them!'

Calypso thought for a moment. 'Do you think Prunella knows about me and Nova?'

'I can't imagine your mother would have told her if they didn't speak to each other.'

'And now we have to invite my evil aunt for tea!'

'That's the plan,' said Alfie.

'If there's an imp involved, the plan will be to cause mischief,' said a deep voice behind them.

The children spun round.

It was the library ghost, standing in his bonnet and dress and tapping an old-fashioned fob watch.

'It's getting late. Go home, Calypso.' He pointed one long finger at the diary in her hands. 'You have found what you were looking for.'

'I'm not sure about that,' replied Calypso. 'My sister is still stuck in that snow globe.'

'Didn't I warn you about imps?' the ghost said to Alfie.

The library lights flickered green.

'Zita must be home!' said Alfie in surprise.

Somewhere in the house a door slammed, and then another.

Gertrude's voice called out, 'Alfie, are you around?'

Then Zita's voice hollered, 'COME HERE NOW, BOY!'

111

That made them all jump – even the ghost.

'What have I done now?' cried Alfie.

'Weren't you supposed to be minding the shop?' suggested the ghost.

Alfie groaned. 'I forgot about the shop! I ran out to help find Nova.'

'Good luck,' whispered the ghost. 'You'll need it, the mood Zita is in.

★

Alfie took a seat at the kitchen table with Gertrude and Zita opposite.

The kitchen was even darker and more cave-like than usual.

The pots were silent on the hob and the day was fading outside the window.

The bug-lights on the walls flickered on.

In their greenish glow, Gertrude's face showed disappointment; Zita's face, anger.

Calypso's face, as she gone off down the path clutching the snow globe containing her sister, had just shown worry.

Alfie was upsetting everyone.

'First the stink bombs and then you leave the shop unattended,' Zita fumed. 'You, boy, are causing nothing but trouble.'

'I'm sorry,' said Alfie. 'There was an emergency.'

Zita narrowed her eyes. 'Explain.'

Alfie hesitated. Should he tell them about the imp in

112

the snow globe and Nova stuck inside and what they had learnt – about his father and Calypso's mother being friends? Maybe his aunts could help them?

But they'd decided to keep it a secret – him and Calypso. They'd both promised not to tell!

'What's the matter?' Zita hissed. 'Tongue tied?'

She took a silver bottle from her pocket and blew a pinch of green powder over Alfie.

'No, Zita!' said Gertrude.

But it was too late.

The powder made Alfie sneeze. Then a terrible queasy feeling came over him. He looked down in horror as a long purple tongue rolled from his mouth to settle, glistening, on his knees. It slithered and twitched and tied itself in a slimy bow.

Magnus, who was hooked upside down on the back of Zita's chair, began to snigger. Rafferty hissed at the bat, his tail swiping the floor.

'STOP THAT SPELL!' shouted Gertrude. 'He's only a boy.'

Zita scowled and muttered something under her breath.

Alfie's tongue returned to normal size. He stuck it out. It was small and pink and fine again.

Zita continued, 'You have no place here. Your father was a birdbrain and your mother was a fool.'

Gertrude nudged Zita sharply.

Zita scowled. 'Well, she was: sausages, lions—'

'What my sister is trying to say, Alfie, is that we've had a trying day and there's a lot going on, so any—'

'Stupidity?' suggested Zita.

'*High spirits*,' said Gertrude. 'Are a bit of a problem. Given our new addition.'

All three of them looked over at the new addition.

It sat in the corner of the kitchen, looking back at them.

It was a plump brown-grey bird with a floaty, wispy tail. On its perch was a sign:

LYREBIRD
PROPERTY OF HEAD WITCH

Below the sign there was a tiny red light and next to that the word:

RECORDING

The lyrebird was listening to every sound they made. Whenever it heard something interesting, it clicked into action, making a whirring noise.

Alfie felt the unfairness of it all.

Here was Zita, who likely had just escaped witch prison thanks to Gertrude, telling *him* off for his mistakes. She had no right to bewitch his tongue!

'Our glorious Head Witch is coming to visit,' said Gertrude, her voice bright and her face worried.

The lyrebird dipped its head, listening carefully. The red RECORDING light flashed.

Gertrude glanced at the lyrebird. 'Aren't we honoured?'

'The Head Witch is coming here?' asked Alfie.

'She fancied a trip to the country.' Zita scowled. 'And she's invited half the witches in the world to join her!'

Alfie didn't have to work out how to ask the Head Witch for tea. She was coming anyway!

Then Alfie had a thought. 'But the Blackstacks and the Morrows—'

The lyrebird listened and whirred on its perch.

'Are the best of friends nowadays!' beamed Gertrude. 'We can't wait to welcome the Head Witch to Switherbroom Hall. Can we, Zita?'

'Mm.'

'Good,' said Gertrude. 'Because she's arriving tomorrow.'

Thoughts were jumping like monkeys in Alfie's head.

The Head Witch was coming to visit.

They had to get her golden key to save Nova!

How could Alfie even begin to sleep?

He crept down the stairs to the kitchen to get himself a drink. As he reached the door, he heard the sound of voices inside. His aunts were still up talking.

'If Prunella catches you—' Gertrude was saying.

'She won't.'

'Do you really want to start a war, Zita?'

There was a pause and then Zita's voice, so cold it sent chills down Alfie's spine.

'If that's what it takes to get rid of Prunella Morrow.'

'She was seemed quite friendly, Zita. She said she never intended to keep you in prison. It was just a warning. All will be forgiven if you stop telling the other witches she's bad.'

Zita made a scoffing noise.

Alfie looked through the crack of the door. The lyrebird was asleep, its eyes closed and head lolling. Rafferty crouched at the foot of its perch with a small silver bottle under his paw. Magnus hung on the perch next to the bird, watching it closely.

They had put the lyrebird to sleep with a spell so they could talk freely without the Head Witch hearing!

'Prunella Morrow has invited herself to our house. Why do you think she's done that, Gertrude?'

Gertrude didn't answer.

'You know why the Head Witch is coming to visit, don't you? She wants what's in our library.' Zita paused. 'I've asked the librarian to increase security for Prunella's arrival.'

Gertrude was thoughtful. 'It's possible. But why wouldn't she just lock us up, storm the library and take it?'

'She knows there are witches who would help us still. But if she succeeds, she will become so powerful no one will dare to fight her.'

Alfie wondered what it was in the library that the Head Witch wanted. An old book perhaps? With difficult, deadly spells in it?

The two witches sat in silence for a long while.

Just when Alfie thought he'd creep back upstairs he heard Gertrude ask . . .

'What about Alfie?'

'He'll have to go,' Zita replied.

'But he's only just arrived!'

'The boy will have to leave for his own safety.'

'But he's made friends with Calypso! According to the childminder, Alfie doesn't usually make friends.'

'He can't be friends with that circus girl. What if she finds out she's a Morrow?'

Too late, thought Alfie. *She already knows.*

Gertrude's voice sounded tired. 'I see your point. Ursula didn't want her girls to know about magic.'

'You should never have let the circus come back here.'

'Perhaps not.'

'After what happened to Ursula,' said Zita quietly.

What happened to Ursula? thought Alfie. *Say it!*

'Do you think her girls are in danger?' asked Gertrude.

'Not if Prunella doesn't know about them,' came Zita's sour answer. 'But if she thought there were other, younger Morrows who might want to take her place one day . . .'

Alfie felt sick – to think his friend could be in danger from the most powerful witch in the world! When just a few days ago neither of them knew anything at all about magic!

There was no telling how mean Prunella could be to her own family – if her diary was anything to go by.

Alfie's aunts sat in silence for a while.

'We'll send the boy to Cousin Pinny.'

117

'Alfie would hate it there!' exclaimed Gertrude. 'She's two hundred years old and lives out on that dreadful island! With all the mud! And not a book in the house! She really does eat slugs and doesn't just pretend to like you do.'

'Do him good.'

'Don't be mean, Zita. And what about Calypso?'

'Mrs Mention gets her way – we send the circus packing.'

Listening at the door, Alfie shook his head. He couldn't imagine hating Zita more.

'Oh no, Zita!'

'Oh *yes*, Gertrude.'

They fell silent for a while.

'The boy leaves tomorrow. There's no other way.'

There was the sound of footsteps across the kitchen floor. Alfie pressed himself behind a hat stand just in time. Zita marched past with Magnus swishing after her.

As Zita climbed the staircase, Alfie saw with a shudder that the snake-headed wooden rail turned green and scaly and its red eyes shone.

CHAPTER 13

The Head Witch

Alfie woke to a frightful noise: the whirring drone of what sounded like . . . a thousand vacuum cleaners.

Alfie jumped from his bed and looked out of the window.

Flying across the rosy-pink, very-early-morning sky were great flocks of . . . *witches*?

Yes, without a doubt, *WITCHES*!

Bobbing through the sky on vacuum cleaners!

Alfie grabbed his father's binoculars and threw open the window.

Most of the witches swayed slowly through the air. The nozzles of their vacuums had reins attached and they rode them as you would a camel or a donkey. Their Familiars rode with them. Alfie spotted fat toads, cats and a startled-looking iguana perched on their witches' shoulders.

A few of the witches wore goggles and helmets. They flew sleek machines and went at staggering speeds. Diving and rising and loop-the-looping, rocketing through the air, leaving twisting trails of green smoke. Their Familiars – fast-flying birds – swooped through the air next to them.

Curiously, the slow-moving witches wore rainbow colours and looked a lot like Gertrude, while the fast and furious witches wore black like Zita.

There were gentlemen witches, too, among the numbers. (Of course some say a girl should be called a witch and a boy should be called a wizard. Nonsense: call yourself whatever you want, be whatever you want: witch or wizard.)

The gentlemen witches wore tweed suits and rode old-fashioned-looking vacuums with gadgets attached. Alfie followed them with his binoculars. Some had straggly beards like Mr Fingerhut and others wore neat moustaches and spectacles. Most of them had a weasel sitting up at the prow.

Their vacuums flew with alarming popping noises and sometimes cut out mid-air, sending the riders spluttering downwards. Now and again Alfie spotted these ancient machines being towed through the sky by other helpful witches.

Alfie wondered what it would be like to fly through the air on such a contraption. He shuddered at the thought of swirling up so high among the birds and the clouds or, worse, plummeting towards the ground!

And now Switherbroom Hall was buzzing with noisy, gabbling witches and the shrieks and grunts and barks of their Familiars.

Perhaps, amid all this chaos, Gertrude would forget to send Alfie away.

Alfie had no intention of being sent to live with Pinny Blackstack to eat slugs on a muddy island.

He was a person, not a parcel!

He would run away with the circus!

He needed to find Calypso and tell her what he had overheard about her wicked Aunt Prunella. After all, Calypso could be in danger!

Alfie quickly got dressed and crept downstairs.

The witches were all talking at once, as witches generally do. Alfie watched in fascination as they blew clouds of green powder on brooms and dusters, which began to furiously sweep and polish all by themselves. This left the witches free to unpack picnic baskets and brew pots of (green) tea and gobble up slices of chocolate cake (with green frosting).

And free to bicker.

The witches were a rowdy lot, as witches usually are. On one side of the house, the witches dressed in black, like Zita, gathered. On the other side, the witches who wore bright colours and had mad hair, like Gertrude, gathered. The gentlemen witches wandered about in the hallway. The witches were all different shapes and sizes, from young to ancient. Only a few of them had warts.

The witches mostly ignored Alfie as he passed, or else they stared at him, or smiled and nodded.

'Have you seen my toad?' asked one witch as he passed by. 'His name is Brian.'

Alfie flinched.

The witch was small and plump like his Aunt Gertrude. Only she had less teeth and her rainbow-patterned trousers were held up with string.

She was wearing a pointed witch's hat. The hat was twitching.

'I haven't, sorry,' said Alfie.

The hat twitched again and then croaked.

'Have you tried looking under your hat?' Alfie suggested.

'Bingo!' cried the witch.

She took off her hat and there on her head sat the biggest toad Alfie had ever seen. The toad looked at him and then licked its own eye.

'EWWW!' exclaimed Alfie.

A nearby witch dressed in black, as tall and thin as his Aunt Zita, only with frizzy silver hair and a rat on her shoulder, started to laugh.

'Moley O'Malley, you numbskull! Your toad is always under your hat!'

'Hester Bodkin, why don't you mind your own business?'

'Excuse me,' said Alfie. 'I'm in a bit of a hurry.'

'Do you want a cuddle of my toad?' asked Moley O'Malley.

Hester Bodkin laughed. 'Or a squeeze of my rat?'

Alfie walked quickly through the house, taking care not to smile or talk to any more witches. He didn't want to cuddle toads or squeeze rats or be turned into a stick or whatever.

Familiars hopped, slithered, fluttered and ran all over the house. There were cats and bats, of course, but Alfie also spotted goats, dogs and a donkey.

And more magical visitors were arriving at every moment. Yet Switherbroom Hall could fit them all inside!

The big house seemed to have got even bigger. The corridors were miles longer with twice as many doors. The staircase was three times as wide. The carpet looked brighter and the walls less cobwebby – and now the wallpaper had a fancy pattern of black and white birds. Ravens and doves! The snake bannister was polished to a shine that matched its gleaming red eyes.

Alfie saw, when he tiptoed past on his way out the back door, that the kitchen was the size of a small cinema, with rows and rows of chairs of different sizes around the fire.

Outside in the garden, it was mayhem.

Witches rushed here and there ordering about bewitched spades and wheelbarrows that frantically dug and trundled. White rose bushes were being planted. A bandstand was being built, along with a huge dovecote. From the cooing coming from the cages on the lawn Alfie was certain doves would feature pretty highly.

Prunella Morrow was on her way!

Alfie heard her name mentioned in the same false bright

way that Gertrude had spoken it. But it was always said with a scowl or a grimace. Alfie began to wonder if anyone liked the Head Witch at all.

Alfie headed towards the circus camp to find Calypso; he was feeling more worried by the moment. What if the circus had already been sent away as Zita had ordered?

Alfie was relieved to find the circus still in the lower field. Calypso was waiting for him outside her bus. She had the snow globe zipped safely into a rucksack. She had heard Nova singing a little while ago. Nova was singing her happy song, said Calypso, who looked anything but happy.

Alfie hardly knew where to start! But he told Calypso all that he'd heard, carefully repeating his aunts' conversation.

Calypso listened to it all gravely, her eyes widening and her face growing pale when she heard that Prunella might have had something to do with her mother's disappearance.

'I want to see the Head Witch arrive,' said Calypso grimly. 'We need to think of a plan – we have to get that golden key and save Nova!'

Alfie hesitated. He would much rather climb into Calypso's bus, lock the doors and keep them both well away from danger!

'Come on, Alfie.' Calypso set out across the field to Switherbroom Hall. 'There's no time to lose.'

Alfie reluctantly followed.

*

Alfie and Calypso hid in a large and leafy bush on the veranda of Switherbroom Hall. No one could see them, but peeping between the branches they had a great view of the landing strip that had appeared across the lawn, fenced off by white rope. Witches were lining up on either side.

Zita and Gertrude were there with their Familiars. Magnus had his claws hooked over Zita's arm like a black leathery umbrella. Rafferty sat at Gertrude's ankles with his ears flat and his tail down.

Zita looked stern and tall in a long gown of black velvet with a high collar. Her black hair was in a bun. Gertrude was wearing her dark green dress, her face pale and her hair bright red.

The lyrebird stood next to them. Still listening to their every word.

The other witches nudged each other and pointed at Zita. Everyone knew she was in *big* trouble for writing about the Head Witch in the newspaper.

But soon enough the witches stopped looking at Zita and started looking up.

In the sky, a shining white dot had appeared and was quickly growing bigger.

A plane! It circled the sky.

The doves in the dovecote began to coo.

The plane came in to land.

The Head Witch had arrived.

'Wow,' whispered Calypso. 'She looks like a newsreader from the telly!'

Alfie nodded. Prunella Morrow was not at all what he expected.

The Head Witch stepped daintily down from the plane, waving at the waiting witches. She had shiny fair hair and a floaty white dress. She had pale pink lipstick and clear blue eyes. When she smiled, which she did often, there were dimples in her cheeks.

'She's lovely!' whispered Calypso. 'It's hard to believe what your aunts said about her – she looks so nice!'

Alfie nodded. How could someone who seemed so happy and friendly be really rotten?

A young witch rushed up and held out a bouquet of white roses to Prunella. As the Head Witch bent to take the flowers, Alfie saw that she was wearing a necklace. On the necklace swung a golden key.

Calypso saw it too. 'The key around her neck – it must be the one!'

Scuttling behind Prunella came a figure in black. Featherlegs, with her rickety legs and headband pulled low.

'Why does she wear that headband, Alfie?'

'To hide her spider's eyes,' said a quiet voice behind them.

Both children jumped.

The library ghost was all but invisible in the sunlight. Alfie could just make out the shape of his bonnet.

'Where you and I have foreheads, Featherlegs has a whole crop of extra eyes,' the ghost continued.

'Oh, that's nasty,' whispered Calypso.

'And she isn't carrying a rucksack, you know,' sniffed the ghost. 'That's her four other limbs folded up behind her.'

Alfie shuddered.

The Head Witch was waving and smiling.

'She seems quite popular,' Alfie said.

'I don't think she is – the witches aren't all smiling back,' noticed Calypso. 'And some of those smiles are pretend.'

Alfie looked closer and saw that Calypso was right. Many of the witches just looked nervous.

A second young witch came forward with a white cardboard box.

'What's in the box, I wonder?' said Alfie.

The library ghost snooped through the branches. 'Cake, if I'm not mistaken.'

Prunella opened the lid and laughed with delight.

'She's easily pleased,' mumbled the ghost. 'It's plain old fruit cake.'

'Oh,' said Alfie. 'That doesn't sound very exciting.'

'The Head Witch loves nothing more than cream cakes,' said the ghost. 'But she's not allowed them – they give her humongous pimples. She has instructed Featherlegs NEVER to let her eat them.'

'Just imagine,' Calypso pondered, 'being able to have all the cream cakes you want – but allowed to eat none of them!'

Alfie glanced at the library ghost. 'The Head Witch is after something in the library; do you know what it is?'

'That's none of your business, Master Blackstack,' the library ghost said sharply. 'You should concentrate on the job you have at hand. Your job is getting hold of that golden key.'

Alfie and Calypso glanced at each other in surprise.

The ghost chuckled. 'Librarians have very good hearing, you know.'

'We don't have a plan,' admitted Alfie glumly.

'Mm,' said the ghost. 'Well, if I were after that key, I'd make sure to get the Head Witch on her own, away from Featherlegs. I don't want to frighten you, but . . .'

'Go on,' said Calypso. 'Please.'

'Featherlegs has been known to eat children.'

'No way!' Calypso cried.

The ghost nodded. 'She spins them up in her web, then bites the top of their heads off, like a boiled egg. Oh, she does like brains, soft and salty!'

Alfie felt sick. 'I don't want to hear any more.'

'So,' continued the ghost, 'if someone were to tempt the Head Witch with the offer of a secret cream cake—'

'She would give Featherlegs the slip,' added Calypso.

'She would!' said the ghost happily.

'Then we could take the key, Alfie!'

'You could, Calypso,' the ghost went on. 'With the Head Witch distracted by a nice juicy cream cake, you could snip the key from her neck. But then you'd need to make your escape. How would you do that?'

Alfie thought a moment. 'I could turn her into a butter dish to give us time to run away?'

'Bravo, Alfie! Now I'm off back to the library. The books misbehave if I leave them alone too long, shuffling about, getting all out of order.' The library ghost lowered his voice. 'Best of luck, been nice knowing you.'

The ghost melted into the wall.

'We could just ask to borrow the golden key,' said Alfie, feeling quite scared now. 'We've never thought of that.'

Calypso laughed. 'And the Head Witch would just lend it to us? She's supposed to be rotten!'

'But isn't it wrong to *pinch* it, Calypso?'

'We'll just be *borrowing* the key, Alfie. We're not keeping it – we only need it to save Nova.'

There was a great cry. The doves were being let out of their baskets. They flew up into the sky in a big cooing cloud. The band struck up with a cheerful tune.

Calypso nudged Alfie. 'We'll go to Mrs Mention's Tea Room. She may be a miserable old trout, but she has the best cream cakes. Prunella Morrow won't be able to resist!'

'Mrs Mention will never sell cakes to us, Calypso!'

'We'll creep in the back way and leave the money on the table.'

Alfie looked doubtful.

'We have to get Nova out, Alfie. This is an emergency!'

'What if we get caught?'

'We can't get caught, Alfie,' said Calypso. 'We just can't.'

CHAPTER 14

A Daring Attempt

The first part of the plan was easy. Alfie and Calypso crept through Mrs Mention's back door and right before them, on the table, was a selection of freshly made cream cakes. Calypso found a box and they put a delicious assortment inside. They left money on the table and rushed back to Switherbroom Hall.

The party was in full swing and more witches were arriving at every moment.

Word had got out that Gertrude and Zita were throwing a big party in honour of the Head Witch. Everyone knew Prunella had invited herself, having no real friends apart from Featherlegs. But witches love a party and don't care who or what it's for.

There were witches and Familiars gossiping in the hallway. There were witches sliding in their socks on the ballroom floor (with their Familiars looking on). There were witches and Familiars dancing on the lawn to the band.

But there was no sign of Gertrude or Zita or Prunella.

The children moved quickly through the house, keeping their heads down.

They ducked into the kitchen and Alfie grabbed the little bottle of green powder from above the cooker and Calypso found a pair of cutters in a toolbox under the sink. They were in a pouch labelled:

ALL-PURPOSE WITCHING SNIPS
For the toughest of toenails (dragons included).
Cut stone, metal, wood and hard cheese
with perfect ease.

'Just the thing!' cried Calypso.

Then they headed for the summerhouse.

The summerhouse had been planted round with roses and given a quick lick of paint for Prunella's visit, but it was still overgrown with brambles and in a quiet corner of the garden.

The children dusted off a deckchair and pulled it next to the table, then laid out Mrs Mention's cakes.

'Do you think we should try a spell, Alfie?' asked Calypso. 'You know, just to make sure we can do it without Gertrude's help?'

'Rafferty helped me before, but there are no cats around just now.'

'Couldn't we use a bug or something?'

'No spiders!' cried Alfie.

Calypso grinned. 'All right, no spiders!'

A quick search of the nearby trees and bushes found a small green friendly looking caterpillar.

They brought it back inside.

Calypso talked to the caterpillar while Alfie thought up the spell.

'It's OK,' she said. 'This is for a good cause and, besides, you need to get used to changing shape. One day you'll be a butterfly.'

The caterpillar gave a wriggle.

'That's the spirit!'

Soon Alfie was ready. Calypso held out the bottle of All-Purpose Witching Powder.

Alfie took a pinch and put it in the palm of his hand.

He blew the powder, closed his eyes and said the words:

Caterpillar very small, the smallest I have seen,
You love crunching leaves in your coat so green.
Help us out with our spell for you are all we've got,
For five seconds – not much more – please be a
*   nice teapot!*

Alfie opened his eyes and looked at the table.

The caterpillar was still a caterpillar.

Nothing had happened.

'I thought you were turning him into a butter dish?' whispered Calypso. 'That worked last time, didn't it?'

'I couldn't find anything to rhyme with "butter dish",' Alfie admitted. 'Maybe I should try again?'

But just as Calypso unstoppered the bottle of All-Purpose Witching Powder . . . the caterpillar hopped right up.

And tumbled straight down.

And twisted all around.

And there was a flash of green light.

The children stared in wonder, for there on the table was a spiky green teapot! It had bristly caterpillar hairs all along the handle.

'You did it, Alfie! You cast an actual spell!'

Alfie laughed. 'I did! I really did!'

The teapot flickered and changed back into a caterpillar.

Calypso clapped her hands. 'My turn!'

Calypso held the sprinkle of All-Purpose Witching Powder in her palm. On the table was a garden snail.

'Ready?' asked Alfie.

He felt a little nervous, mostly because Calypso wouldn't tell him her spell. She had worked on it carefully while she was looking under logs and in bushes.

Calypso blew the powder and said the words:

Snail round and fine with horns or eyes I really
  cannot tell,
You have a squidgy body and a lovely twisty shell.
You live in slimy buckets and like crawling in the
  rain,
But be a pal, for half a min, and turn into a train!

Alfie looked at the snail in alarm.

A train!

Inside the summerhouse!

He thought of the size of the Tube trains in London.

'A *train*, Calypso?' he groaned.

Calypso bit her lip.

The snail hopped and spun and there was a flash of green.

There on the table stood a model of an old-fashioned train, small and snail-patterned, with whorls from its wheels to its funnel.

Calypso let out a sigh of relief and began to laugh.

If they didn't have the small matter of getting hold of the Head Witch's golden key and saving Nova – well, they could have spent hours practising their new skill.

'We're as ready as we'll ever be,' said Alfie. 'We have the cakes, the spell – everything. All we need is the Head Witch.'

'I'll go and get her,' said Calypso. 'You look too worried; your face will give the game away.'

Alfie tried to make his face look less worried. 'No, I'll go – it was my fault with the snow globe—'

'This is no one's fault, Alfie!' said Calypso. 'Other than that imp, and perhaps Mr Fingerhut for giving you the snow globe in the first place.'

From outside came the sound of a band striking up another noisy number.

Calypso ducked out the door. 'I'll be back soon. Just you practise that spell.'

*

Alfie waited in the summerhouse. First, he rearranged the cakes, then he sat on the deckchair, then he went outside to look out for Calypso.

Alfie had just about given up hope when he saw Calypso returning across the lawn. The Head Witch was with her, just the two of them alone, with no sign of Featherlegs.

They were both laughing. The Head Witch in her floaty white dress, with her shiny newsreader hair. Calypso in her shorts, with her hair scooped into a messy ponytail.

They looked a lot alike.

Prunella Morrow swept into the summerhouse. When she saw Alfie, her smile disappeared. 'Who might you be?'

In his confusion, Alfie gave a little bow. 'Shane, Your Highness.'

'Shane?' Prunella raised one eyebrow, looking like Calypso at her most uppity.

'Shane's my friend,' said Calypso.

'Well, if you're Kitty's friend . . .'

Alfie and Calypso had decided to give the Head Witch false names – otherwise she'd know who had turned her into a butter dish.

The Head Witch smiled frostily. 'We're going to eat some secret cakes! What fun.'

Alfie pointed at the cakes on the table. 'Mrs Mention's finest selection!'

'Her creamiest and best!' added Calypso.

'Florence Mention may be a perfect dragon,' said Prunella, 'but she makes the best cakes in the world!'

'You know Mrs Mention?' asked Alfie in surprise.

'Let's just say we're old friends.' Prunella narrowed her eyes. 'Exactly *why* are you offering me secret cream cakes, children? You're not trying to *trick* me, are you?'

'No!' exclaimed Calypso, her face reddening. 'I mean, don't you like cream cakes?'

'I do, but they don't like me.'

Prunella settled in the deckchair, smoothing down her white dress and shaking back her fair curls. She straightened her necklace and patted the golden key.

'Pass me that plate, boy. Be quick about it.'

Alfie offered her the plate and the Head Witch selected a lovely plump chocolate éclair. 'Now, *you* bite into it.'

'Excuse me?' said Alfie.

'I want to make sure it's not bewitched, Shane,' she replied. 'Believe it or not, I have many enemies.'

Alfie took a bite and the Head Witch watched closely.

'Good,' she finally said. 'You're still a boy and not an earwig. I shall have a cake!'

'Oh, do!' encouraged Calypso.

The Head Witch selected a cream scone. She licked her lips. 'You're very bad for me, cake, but I'll eat you anyway.'

Alfie glanced nervously at Calypso. She was holding the All-Purpose Witching Snips ready. As soon as she'd cut off the necklace, Alfie would turn the Head Witch into a butter dish and they would make a quick getaway with the golden key before she changed back again. They would release Nova and Alfie would run away with the circus.

He'd repeated the spell to himself over and over. They'd

136

changed the words a bit because Prunella wasn't a cat and Calypso had found a rhyme for "butter dish":

Head Witch in floaty dress so fair,
With fab lipstick, shoes and hair.
Grant us, do, our one big wish:
For five minutes be a butter dish!

Alfie hoped it would work.

Prunella closed her eyes, opened her mouth and took a bite.

Calypso took a step nearer, snips ready in her hand, her eyes on the chain around the Head Witch's neck from which the golden key hung.

Alfie took the bottle of All-Purpose Witching Powder from his pocket and unstoppered it.

Prunella chewed her cake with her eyes closed, making happy noises.

She seemed completely distracted, but when Calypso's snips neared her neck, Prunella's eyes flew open.

Calypso hid the snips behind her back.

In his surprise, Alfie accidentally dropped the bottle of green powder.

Calypso quickly kicked the bottle under the deckchair.

The Head Witch watched the children closely as she finished the last of her cake. She licked her fingers.

'I'd better be going soon. Featherlegs will be worried.' She smiled. 'Did you know she was a spider once upon a time?'

'Was she?' said Calypso.

'Just as well you didn't try to trick me,' continued Prunella. 'If anyone tries to trick me, Featherlegs winds them in her web and bites them. Her bites are very poisonous, you know.'

The Head Witch selected another cream cake. 'One bite from Featherlegs and you'd turn blue and your fingers and toes would fall off and your eyes would become marbles. Soon you would be deader than a doorknob.'

Calypso glanced at Alfie.

'What's worse,' the Head Witch went on, 'what's *far* worse, is that sometimes Featherlegs doesn't wait for her prey to be *dead* before she eats them. She always starts by cracking open their heads like soft-boiled eggs.'

Alfie fought the urge to run away – what the library ghost had said was true!

'Which is why it's always better not to try to trick me.' Prunella patted her lips delicately with a handkerchief. 'Well, that was yum. By the way, what do you think of my shoes?'

'Your shoes?' asked Calypso.

'Yes, my shoes and my hair?'

'You're asking us?' said Alfie.

Prunella nodded. 'You both look fashionable.'

Alfie had to stop himself from laughing out loud.

'All the other witches tell me I look fashionable because I'm the boss.'

Calypso looked at Prunella's white pointy shoes, then

at her hair, which had curls big and round enough to roll around a baked bean can.

'I *suppose* you're fashionable,' answered Calypso. 'Only . . .'

'Only what?' asked Prunella.

'Trainers might be nicer and maybe a ponytail,' suggested Calypso. 'A bit more casual and less . . . news-reader.'

Alfie stared at Calypso. Was she trying to get them eaten by Featherlegs?

To his surprise, however, the Head Witch smiled. She stood up and hooked her handbag over her arm.

'Would you like a job, Kitty?' she asked Calypso.

'What sort of job?'

Prunella's smile widened. 'You're not part of the cele-brations here, are you?'

'Oh no. We just brought the cakes,' said Calypso.

'And what lovely cakes!' Prunella held out her hand to Calypso. 'Your new job is simply to be my friend. It would be lovely to have nice *honest* companion who knows about trainers and ponytails and brings me secret cakes.'

Calypso hesitated. Then she stepped forward and took Prunella's hand.

Prunella turned to Alfie. 'You seem like a nice chap, Shane, but I don't like boys. No offence.'

Alfie stood speechless.

'You don't mind if I borrow your chum, do you?' asked Prunella.

139

Alfie managed to shake his head.

'Good.' The Head Witch turned back to Calypso and lowered her voice. 'Today's celebrations are strictly off-limits to the non-magical – but I have a feeling that you know a *teeny tiny* bit about magic, don't you?'

Calypso nodded very slightly.

'Good.' Prunella giggled. 'Then let me give you a magical disguise!'

Prunella opened her handbag and took out a fancy silver bottle. She sprinkled green powder on the palm of her hand and blew it over Calypso.

Alfie looked at his friend in astonishment. She was no longer Calypso.

A neat, sleek young witch stood in Calypso's place. With shiny brushed hair and a white dress just like Prunella's.

'Try it my way today!' laughed Prunella.

The neat young witch frowned and scratched her head, which instantly made her look more like Calypso.

Prunella swept out of the summerhouse. 'Come, Kitty!'

Calypso followed, stopping to whisper to Alfie, 'I'll get the key. Just you wait and see!'

Alfie waited in the lower field. He had Calypso's rucksack on. He wore it to the front so he could keep an eye on the snow globe; he had minded it carefully while Calypso was off with the Head Witch.

Alfie sat on the wall and worried. It was a good spot for worrying. He could see all the way down to Calypso's bus and all the way up to Switherbroom Hall. There was no sign of Calypso leaving the party. From the wall it looked like a nice normal summer bash was going on up at the house: bunting fluttering around gazebos and the sounds of laughter and music.

Was Alfie the only person to have noticed a couple of hundred witches flying over Little Snoddington on vacuum cleaners? Maybe the villagers hadn't been awake, or hadn't believed their eyes and ears? Or maybe the witches used magic to hide what they were up to? What an idea! Imagine looking up into the sky and seeing just clouds when there are really hundreds of witches flying over your head!

For most of the day Alfie had followed and watched as Calypso had moved about the house at Prunella's side. Alfie was good at going unnoticed. He was careful to hide from his aunts too, although they seemed to be too caught up in the Head Witch's visit to bother about him.

All eyes were on Prunella, and if they weren't on Prunella, they were on Zita. Alfie listened to the witches gossiping as he hid under tables and behind curtains.

A big fight was brewing: some thought Prunella would win, others thought Zita.

There was a formal luncheon in the ballroom with candlesticks and golden plates. Then there was the best Familiar competition, with first prize going to a large and hissy swan. There was a poetry competition, with all the poems written on the subject of the Head Witch's complete brilliance.

Zita scoffed at the poems. Gertrude nudged her.

Alfie wondered how it would all end.

Calypso, on the other hand, didn't seem to have a trouble in the world!

She sat laughing and smiling with Prunella. They even linked arms as they went about Switherbroom Hall.

Alfie had never linked arms with Calypso.

Did she still care about saving Nova?

He would ask her now.

Calypso was coming wandering, humming, down the field. Her magical glossy witch disguise had worn off a little, her scruffy ponytail was back and she had tomato ketchup down her front.

'Did you get the golden key?' Alfie asked.

Calypso stopped humming. 'Nope. Didn't get the chance.'

'But you were with Prunella all afternoon!'

'What was I supposed to do?' asked Calypso. 'Grab it from her neck? With that spider creature and all those witches watching?'

Alfie was silent. She had a point.

'Anyway,' said Calypso. 'I think we should tell her.'

'Tell her what?'

'About Nova and the imp in the snow globe.' She paused. 'And that she's my aunt.'

Alfie had a sudden sneaking feeling. 'You've already told her everything!'

Calypso reddened. 'I have not! But I think we should. Prunella would help us.'

'But she's really bad! I told you what my aunts said about her!'

Calypso shrugged. 'Maybe they got it wrong. She seems all right – she's fun.'

'Fun?'

Calypso nodded, her eyes bright. 'She magicked up this rainbow candyfloss and she says she's going to take me up in her plane. She's going to let me fly it!'

'Tremendous.'

'You would hate it, Alfie. It will go so brilliantly high!'

'I'm OK with planes.' It was Alfie's turn to redden. The last time his father had taken him on one of his trips Alfie had sat quivering and holding the flight attendant's hand. For *three* hours.

'What if Prunella is tricking you?' Alfie said. 'Pretending to be nice when she's wicked. Just like the White Witch. But instead of offering you Turkish delight she's buying your friendship with plane rides and candy-floss!'

'She's not buying me with anything,' Calypso snapped. 'And I don't even know what you're talking about with this "White Witch" stuff.'

'The White Witch from *The Lion, the Witch and the Wardrobe*; it's a book.'

'Haven't heard of it.'

'It's famous!' said Alfie, exasperated. 'Don't you read?'

Calypso scowled at him. 'I'm a great one for reading!

143

I just don't walk around all the time with my nose stuck in a book!'

'No, you just walk around all the time with your nose stuck up in the air!' Alfie jumped off the wall and gave a bow. 'I'm Calypso, look at me, I'm good at *everything*.'

He instantly regretted it when he saw Calypso's face.

'Why are you being mean to me, Alfie?'

He kicked the wall. It hurt his toe.

Why was he being mean? Because he was angry: they were supposed to be in this together. Now Calypso was changing their plan and making decisions without him. He might as well go and live with Pinny Blackstack and eat slugs for ever and ever.

Alfie suddenly felt very alone.

He had always been alone in a way. Even his parents hadn't liked him that much – at least, not enough to spend time with him.

Even so, he missed them. Sometimes Alfie couldn't quite believe his mother and father were never coming back. It was easier to imagine that they were away on some dangerous adventure involving wild beasts and huffy birds.

Now Calypso, the only friend he'd ever had, was looking at him like he was a bug in her ice cream sundae!

'Tell Prunella who you are, see if I care!' he cried. 'I'll be living on some mud island soon anyway.'

Calypso's eyes flashed. 'It's *my* sister who's been kidnapped! Give me back that rucksack; you've already lost that snow globe once!'

144

Alfie took off the rucksack and handed it to her.

'And if I want to ask Aunt Prunella for help, I will,' Calypso went on. 'I'm sure she'd get Nova out in a flash!'

'Oh, "*Aunt* Prunella", is it? What about her diary – the things she did to your mother? Ursula hated her!'

'That was when they were younger – no one likes their sister when they are kids!'

'YOU like *your* sister!' Alfie shouted.

'That's not the POINT!' Calypso shouted back.

Alfie took a deep breath and tried again. 'Have you forgotten what my aunts said: that Prunella had something to do with your mother's disappearance?'

'They're Blackstacks – of course they'd say horrible things about Prunella.' Calypso turned and strode off across the field. 'Morrows and Blackstacks are enemies!'

Alfie watched her go, his heart plummeting.

What should he do now?

He waited by the wall for a while, just in case Calypso calmed down and came back.

It got dark and a bit cold.

Alfie trudged back to Switherbroom Hall.

In his troubled mood, he hadn't noticed the faint scuffling behind the wall where he had sat. Someone or something even better at going unnoticed than Alfie had been hiding there.

The figure straightened its cloak and headband, patted the hump on its back and set off across the field with a smile on its long, thin face.

It was not a nice smile.

CHAPTER 15

Zita in Trouble!

As night fell, the witches up at Switherbroom Hall continued celebrating, only quietly. The Head Witch announced she was having an early night and climbed aboard her plane. The ladder was pulled up after her, but her plane stayed parked outside the house.

The news was that Prunella had decided to stay for a few days. So the visiting witches would all be staying too – they didn't want to miss a good fight!

Tents were put up on the lawn and fires lit under cauldrons. Inside Switherbroom Hall, every bed, chair and window ledge was taken. Witches shook out green-and-black striped sleeping bags and cosied down with their Familiars.

The ghostly librarian had locked the library doors. He would not permit any witches to sleep in his library.

Alfie couldn't even think of sleeping.

He lay on his bed with his eyes wide open.

Would Calypso tell Prunella everything?

Would Prunella help Calypso to get Nova back?

Would he be shipped off to Pinny Blackstack's tomorrow?

The big house was silent.

He still had to return the bottle of All-Purpose Witching Powder he'd taken from the kitchen. Everyone would surely be asleep by now.

Alfie tiptoed through the house to the kitchen, stepping over snoring witches. Two bats raced each other up and down the hallway, until soft whistles from their witches brought them back to nestle under blankets or hang from a curtain pole.

A light was still on in the kitchen. Alfie peeped through the door. Gertrude and Zita were sitting at the table with Rafferty and Magnus next to them. All of them were peering into a large bowl placed in the middle of the table.

The lyrebird was asleep on its perch in the corner of the room.

Alfie moved nearer, setting the door creaking. Gertrude looked up. She held a finger over her mouth and beckoned Alfie forward.

Zita scowled at him, then returned her attention to the bowl on the table.

With horror, Alfie saw that the bowl was full of water and in that water wriggled a tangle of worms.

The worms were making patterns.

Not just patterns . . . the worms were making words!

Zita tapped the water in the bowl with a pen.

Alfie read:

We are being listened to
Not just by the Lyrebird
Prunella is up to no good. Why was Calypso with
her?

Alfie frowned.

Zita tapped again:

Spill it, Alfie
We knew it was Calypso – it wasn't much of a
disguise

Gertrude passed a pen to Alfie. He looked at it. Zita rolled her eyes and tapped her pen on the water:

Think of what you want to say and the worms
will write it
Twit

Letters delivered by ravens, messages from imps and now word-worms! Why couldn't anyone communicate normally when magic was involved?

Zita tapped again:

Why are you still here, boy?

Gertrude took Zita's pen and tapped:

*Alfie, it might be best if you stayed somewhere
   else for a while
Things are HOTTING up with Prunella around*

Zita grabbed the pen from Gertrude and tapped:

Blah. Blah. Blah. What was circus girl DOING?

Alfie thought very carefully about what he wanted to say
and what he *didn't* want to say.

He touched his pen to the water. The worms squirmed
and made a sentence:

Calypso knows Prunella is her aunt

Zita and Gertrude looked startled. The bat rustled his
wings and the cat flattened his ears. Alfie quickly touched
the water again:

*Prunella doesn't know who Calypso is
She thinks her name is Kitty*

Zita breathed out and tapped her pen in the water:

Keep it that way

Prunella has turned most of her family into pebbles

Alfie replied:

Is that what happened to Calypso's mum?

Zita tapped the water again:

More or less

Alfie had to talk to Calypso again, to warn her. Only Calypso was probably not his friend any more, if she ever had been. He looked down at the worms. He hadn't meant to tap the water!

I have no friends

Alfie's cheeks burned red with shame. Zita looked away, while her bat tucked his head under his wing and started snuffling there. Gertrude patted Alfie's arm sympathetically and Rafferty licked his hand.

Somehow, Alfie felt, the sympathy was worse.

It was very late at night when Alfie heard a noise at his window. It sounded like wet washing flapping.

He got out of bed and drew back the curtain. He could see by the moonlight that there was an umbrella trying to get in.

150

Magnus the bat was looking in through the window, red-eyed and terrible.

Alfie dived back into bed, willing the bat to go away.

The tapping got louder.

Alfie pulled a pillow over his head.

The tapping got louder still. Then the tapping turned into the screeching of claw against windowpane.

Alfie got up and opened the window.

The bat flew in, circled the room, dropped something on the bed and flitted out of the window.

Alfie switched on his torch and shone it on the bed.

He saw with relief that it was only a leaflet!

The FACTS about your HEAD WITCH that she DOESN'T WANT YOU TO KNOW

The leaflet said that it was time for a change. That it was unfair for ONE witch to make up the rules for EVERY WITCH. (And who were these rules best for? The Head Witch, of course!)

The Head Witch should listen to what all the other witches wanted. All witches should be able to speak freely and not be sent to prison for disagreeing with the Head Witch. Newspapers should not be banned for telling the truth about the Head Witch.

Enough was enough!

There were witches brave enough to stand up to the Head Witch. They were looking for others to join them.

OUT WITH THE HEAD WITCH!

Alfie folded up the leaflet, which promptly exploded in a puff of green smoke.

He looked out of the window at the plane on the lawn – the lights were out on board. All around, witches and Familiars were asleep in their tents. And above the tents, Alfie could make out a dark fluttering. He grabbed his father's binoculars and by the light of the moon saw that Magnus was not alone – bats filled the sky! They were dropping leaflets all over the grounds of Switherbroom Hall!

Alfie caught sight of a shadowy shape scuttling under the wings of the plane.

Featherlegs!

She had dropped to her hands and feet and was gathering up the leaflets. Crawling and jumping over the lawn and bushes and up onto the roof of a gazebo! Moving faster than any human could!

Alfie shivered and quickly drew the curtains.

★

Alfie woke to the sound of helicopters.

Helicopters. Really?

It was early morning, the start of another fine summer's day.

Sleek white helicopters were landing near Prunella's plane, their whirring blades slowing to a halt. They had the sign of the white dove on their tail fins.

Witches struggled out of tents or wandered out of the house bleary-eyed. Familiars stretched and ran and slithered or shook out their wings.

Guards jumped out of the helicopter – at least they looked like guards or soldiers, with their white caps and white uniforms. They might have been witches, but they were dressed very differently from the witches Alfie had seen so far.

The guards marched up to the house. The witches shrank back as they passed.

Alfie watched with horror as the guards pushed a young witch out of their way and shouted at an ancient tortoise Familiar who had bumbled across their path. The gathered witches saw it too. There was a tense and deadly silence.

A few pointed up at the plane. The door had opened and Prunella stood on the steps in a floaty white nighty, smiling and holding a pair of binoculars.

The guards stamped into Switherbroom Hall.

Alfie felt fear in the bottom of his stomach.

Was this what the beginning of a Witch War looked like?

Alfie pulled up the hood of his anorak and walked quickly through the house. Groups of witches were huddled together, whispering. He went out of the back door and into the garden and crept inside the bush on the veranda. Alfie watched through the branches as something horrid happened right before his eyes.

Zita, in a black robe and black slippers, was being marched out of the house. On each side of her was a stern-faced guard. Another guard walked behind holding a pillowcase by the neck; something spiky was inside fighting to get out. Magnus the bat! Another guard carried a pile of leaflets – just like the one Magnus had dropped on Alfie's bed.

Gertrude watched too, from the side of the path, wiping her eyes on the sleeve of her rainbow-striped dressing gown. Some of the witches shook their heads as Zita passed. She didn't seem to notice; her face was like stone. She was pushed into a helicopter. Then one by one the helicopters took off and flew up into the sky and over Switherbroom Hall.

The Head Witch waved cheerily at the departing helicopters, then stepped back into her plane, Featherlegs scampering behind.

Everyone waited. But the plane didn't take off.

The Head Witch, it seemed, was in no hurry to leave Switherbroom Hall. Neither were the visiting witches. No one wanted to miss out on any news about Zita. The older witches lit fires under cauldrons and settled down to brew tea and do jigsaws. The younger witches made up dance routines and played with their Familiars.

At least with the Head Witch staying, Alfie might have another chance to try to get the golden key. But he couldn't think of one good plan that didn't end with him becoming a spider snack.

He needed to see Calypso. Whether she was the Head

Witch's new best friend or not, she was in danger! If Prunella had made her own sister vanish, what was to say she wouldn't do the same to her niece?

Alfie headed down to the circus camp.

He could see Calypso's bus in the distance. Calypso was probably asleep in her bunk. Or maybe she was awake thinking about her new fun Aunt Prunella and how terrific she was. Or maybe Calypso was peering into the snow globe, worrying about how to save her sister. Alfie had no idea how Calypso was keeping Nova's disappearance secret from the circus folk.

It suddenly struck Alfie that there was a lot he didn't know about Calypso's life. He thought about how some of the people in the village treated her: as if she was worse than them because she lived on a bus. He'd been mean to her too.

So what if Calypso hadn't heard of the White Witch? She was clever and brave and no doubt knew a hundred things he didn't. While Alfie had spent his life hiding from danger and reading sneaked-in library books in his bedroom, Calypso had travelled far and wide!

Alfie felt small and mean and sorry. There was only one thing for it: he had to set things right.

Granny Fagan was up early. She came creaking in her motorbike leathers around Calypso's bus with a pipe stuck in the corner of her mouth.

She nodded at him, eyes twinkly in a wrinkly face. 'Alfie.'

'Have you seen Calypso?' He pointed to the bus. 'There doesn't seem to be anyone in.'

Granny Fagan shook her head. 'They're up and out early again today, her and Nova, with the bunks made. I haven't seen those kids in days!'

'Do you know where she might be?' asked Alfie.

'I don't.' Granny Fagan squinted at him. 'You look just like your Aunt Zita.'

'Not my father then?' muttered Alfie.

'Calypso's mother and your father were best friends, did you know that?'

Alfie nodded. 'Ursula and Phineas.'

Granny Fagan struck a match and lit her pipe. She looked at him slyly. 'Of course, now and again they fought.'

'They fought?'

'They did. Friends fight all the time, Alfie.'

'Surely best friends never fight?'

'A best friend is for life.' Granny Fagan smiled. 'A few fights won't change that.'

Alfie wondered if he shouldn't tell Granny Fagan everything. She was tough and clever and might just know what to do.

'Do you know about magic?' he ventured.

Granny Fagan nodded. 'A bit. I also know that Ursula didn't want the magic life. But we came back to this village every year so that she could see Gertrude. They became great friends too. Especially when Ursula wasn't allowed to see your father any more.'

Alfie thought for a moment. 'You wouldn't happen to know anything about imps and Head Witches, would you?'

Granny Fagan smiled so that her fierce little eyes all but disappeared in her wrinkly face. 'No – and I don't want to.'

Alfie smiled back.

'Calypso thinks very highly of you, you know,' said Granny Fagan. 'She rarely makes friends.'

'Really?' said Alfie, his heart lifting.

'Really. Now, stay out of trouble, Alfie Blackstack. And if you find those girls, you let me know.' Granny Fagan stuck her pipe back in her mouth and creaked off round the bus.

There was no sign of Calypso anywhere about the camp. Children and dogs ran here and there, people sat chatting and drinking tea. Alfie plucked up courage and asked a few of the circus folk if they'd seen Calypso, but no one had. He started to feel more and more worried. What if the Head Witch had stolen her? Or what if Calypso was avoiding him?

Alfie was so busy worrying he walked straight into Shane Fagan.

Shane grabbed Alfie by the shoulder and pushed him behind a parked van.

The older boy had added a studded leather belt to his black jeans and T-shirt. He had a tattoo drawn on his arm in biro. Which almost made Alfie laugh. Only the expression on Shane's face wasn't funny.

Besides, Shane had friends with him.

One held a cricket bat and the other had a long key chain, which he flicked menacingly.

'You got Calypso into trouble up at the tea room,' Shane growled. 'Now that old lady says we have to leave town.'

Shane's friends spat on the grass.

'First you scare my horse and then you wreck our show.' Shane's eyes flashed. 'You make me sick, skulking around, blinking behind them glasses.'

'I'm sorry—'

In one deft move, Shane snatched Alfie's glasses off his face.

'Please! I can't see!'

Shane threw Alfie's glasses on the ground. The others laughed. Alfie's eyes stung with tears. He twisted and tried to get out of Shane's grasp, half hoping Calypso was nearby, half hoping she wasn't.

Alfie had been bullied before, of course. A few children had laughed at his anorak or called him names. But no one had ever pushed him and taken his glasses!

And these boys were much bigger than him. This wasn't fair! A tiny flash of bravery sparked deep in Alfie.

'Let me go,' he shouted at Shane. 'Let me go, you big, ugly bully!

Shane stopped in amazement. But not at Alfie's words.

Rolling along the ground, straight towards Shane, was the snow globe. It was glowing green. From this strange object came the sound of *muttering*.

Shane frowned and glanced at his friends. They were

158

staring at the snow globe, their mouths open and their eyes wide.

The snow globe jumped up and banged down on the toe of Shane's trainer. Again and again!

'Oww!' cried Shane. 'Get it off me!'

From the snow globe came the sound of *jeering*.

The snow globe backed up and began to circle around Shane. It gathered speed until it became a green shouting blur. Then it jumped up high off the ground – and hit Shane squarely on the nose!

Shane screamed and put his hands up to his face.

Alfie grabbed his glasses and scrambled to his feet. He pushed past the shocked circus boys and didn't stop running until he was deep among the trees.

It took Alfie a while to stop shaking and get his breath back, and when he did he saw that the snow globe had followed him into the forest. It nudged his foot fondly, like a pet dog.

Alfie picked up the snow globe. 'Thanks, I think. Although you shouldn't really have whacked Shane Fagan on the nose!'

From inside the snow globe: chuckling.

'I thought you were with Calypso. Do you know where she is?' Alfie asked.

The snow blizzard cleared. Alfie saw yellow eyes blinking on the other side of the glass. Then the face moved out of the way.

Behind the imp was Mrs Mention's Tea Room.

CHAPTER 16

Truth in a Teacup

Little Snoddington was all of a fluster. It wasn't every day that a *celebrity* came to the village – and now, rumour had it, a star of daytime television had stopped by for elevenses at Mrs Mention's! Crowds began to gather outside the tea room. Some wore their best hats and clutched autograph books. Many turned giddy at the sight of the shiny white limousine parked on the high street. No one noticed a figure in black scuttle round the back of the tea room (and run straight up the wall to pry in through the windows). They only had eyes for the celebrity.

But the oddest thing was that when they went to spread the word about the celebrity – *no one could remember her name!*

Mrs Mention seated the celebrity and her charming

young friend – a nice girl in a neat white dress – next to the window so that passers-by could clearly see that she had very important customers.

The celebrity even posed for a photograph with Mrs Mention and gave a quote for the local paper:

Mrs Mention's cakes are delish.

All of the tables were quickly taken in the tea room. The rest of the villagers had to queue outside and gawk in through the windows.

The stranger could *only* be a celebrity.

So glossy and smiling! So perfect, from the tip of her ponytail to the toes of her sparkling white trainers! And with her a smart young girl – a mini version!

The celebrity ordered an Elegant Elevenses Super-Lush Selection for two, much to Mrs Mention's approval. All the customers in the tearoom promptly ordered exactly the same. Apart from Mrs Vicar, who ordered what she always had for elevenses, celebrity or no celebrity: a glass of bitter lemon and a rock cake.

Prunella settled back in her chair and smiled across her teacup at Calypso. 'My darling Kitty, it's wonderful that you could join me.' She lowered her voice. 'Pretend all these cream cakes are yours when Featherlegs comes back.'

Mrs Mention came over to the table carrying a teapot. She set the teapot down and fussed over spoons and napkins.

She curtsied. 'Will there be anything else, madam?'

'No, thank you, Mrs Mention, this is perfect!' Prunella smiled warmly.

Mrs Mention nodded, smiling back. Her smile fell as she turned to Calypso. 'Do I know you?'

Calypso shook her head.

'Thank you, Mrs Mention,' said Prunella. 'We'll let you know if we need anything else.'

Mrs Mention wandered back behind the counter, where she stood watching Calypso with narrowed eyes.

Prunella opened her handbag. 'I feel your disguise may be wearing thin, my dove.' She took out a tiny ruby-red bottle and pulled out the stopper. 'You said Mrs Mention wouldn't allow you in here before, just because you wore trainers?'

'She's very strict.'

'I can't believe that! Because I'm wearing trainers now!'

Calypso blushed. She tried to think quickly. 'But you look like a film star.'

Prunella smiled. 'Are you being quite honest with me, Kitty?'

Calypso nodded, blushing deeper.

'Very good,' nodded Prunella. 'Let's top up your disguise – into your tea, yes? One, two, three drops.'

Calypso watched her tea turn bubble-gum pink. 'What happened to the green powder?'

'All out of green powder; this does exactly the same job. Drink up, darling! We wouldn't want Mrs Mention to recognise you as a trainer-wearer!'

Calypso sipped her tea. It had a hint of strawberry.

'Go on, Kitty, finish up your tea and then you can have another cup! And a cake! Would you like a cake?'

'I'd like to eat all of them,' Calypso said bluntly. Her eyes widened with surprise.

Prunella giggled.

Calypso put down her cup. She suddenly felt weird: hot and cold and dizzy and excited all at once, with butterflies in her tummy and a foggy feeling in her brain. She looked at Prunella.

'I don't think you shouldn't eat any more cream cakes, on account of those big pimples on your nose. I saw you squeezing them. Pop, pop – it was disgusting.'

Prunella stopped laughing.

'Sorry!' cried Calypso, putting her hand over her mouth. 'Actually, I'm not sorry at all,' she mumbled through her fingers.

Prunella took hold of Calypso's hand. 'It's OK. Tell me everything, my love. It will make you feel so much better!'

'I hate Mrs Mention and all these twittering old ladies!' Calypso blurted out.

She looked around in panic. The other customers were no doubt listening in – nosy buzzards that they were!

But Calypso saw that the room was now darker – why, all the curtains had all been drawn! And there was something oddly different about the people in Mrs Mention's Tea Room.

Mrs Vicar seemed to be growing into her chair. Her sour face was now a fresh shade of green. Tendrils peeped from the cuffs of her cardigan where her hands used to be.

Mrs Vicar was transforming into a plant! They all were!

Their faces were turning green and their heads were sprouting leaves.

Calypso leapt to her feet in horror and then sat down again. The room was spinning – everything was swimming before her eyes.

She felt very scared.

She was changing too!

She began to cry. 'I'm turning into a plant!'

Prunella laughed. 'Don't be silly, Kitty!'

Calypso checked her own hands: she still had fingers. Her face reflected in Mrs Mention's best silver teapot didn't seem green.

Looking around she realised – with a scream of fright – that she and Prunella were the only people in the room now. In place of Mrs Mention's customers sat potted plants. Plants of all kinds: small and tufty, big and spiky, graceful and leafy. And next to the plants lay crumpled piles of cardigans and spectacles, handbags and false teeth.

'I don't feel well,' Calypso said. 'I'm seeing things!'

'Oh dear,' smiled Prunella slyly. 'Perhaps you've drunk something peculiar?'

'Everyone is a plant!'

'Yes, they are!' beamed Prunella. 'And isn't it pleasantly quiet without all that gossiping?'

Calypso stared at her. 'You did it! Oh, how wicked!'

'I'm wonderfully wicked!' Prunella clapped her hands happily. 'That's one of my top secrets! Have *you* got any secrets?'

Calypso shook her head, but she felt the truth bubbling up from deep inside her like a big burp.

Prunella took firm hold of Calypso's hands to stop her from covering her mouth.

All Calypso's secrets came tumbling out.

Calypso told Prunella about the snow globe and Nova's disappearance and the deal made with the imp and the plot to snatch Prunella's golden key and finding Prunella's old diary that was lost in the forest and reading it and that her name was Calypso, not Kitty, and she was Ursula's daughter.

'Goodo,' said Prunella. 'I thought you had a few things that you wanted to get off your chest.'

Calypso sat with her head held low. Tears fell on the skirt of her nice white dress. She had all but run out of secrets.

Prunella smiled. 'You've been a very naughty girl, Calypso. But you didn't plan to steal my golden key all by yourself, did you?'

Calypso closed her eyes. She felt dizzy and sick and scared.

'Look at me, girl!' hissed Prunella.

Calypso opened her eyes. The Head Witch's smiles and dimples had vanished; in their place was a terrifying frosty-eyed glare.

'That boy – Shane was his name, wasn't it? Who is Shane really?'

Calypso felt her lips twitch with the effort of not telling the truth.

Prunella banged the table. 'Hurry up! I haven't got all day!'

Calypso shook her head.

'All right then, how would you like to be an earwig?' said the Head Witch icily. 'Or better still, half an earwig.'

Prunella blew green powder over Calypso, then rhymed a few words and BAM!

Calypso looked down in horror. Her tummy was covered with big coppery scales. Two extra arms had appeared at either side. She waggled them – oh heavens, they belonged to her!

Calypso screamed.

Prunella laughed.

All around her, potted plants, once tea-drinking villagers, trembled. They could do nothing to save Calypso.

'If you don't answer my question,' said Prunella, 'you'll stay like that for ever. Once more: who is the boy?'

'Alfie Blackstack,' Calypso replied miserably. 'The snow globe is his.'

The scales and extra arms disappeared, she was fully herself again.

Prunella gave a hoot. 'A Blackstack! You're just like your stupid mother – you think your enemy is your friend!'

'My mum wasn't stupid!'

Prunella ignored her. 'Where did Alfie Blackstack get this snow globe? From his aunts?'

Calypso shook her head. 'Mr Fingerhut.'

'That old troublemaker!' Prunella muttered. Then she looked thoughtful. 'This snow globe, what does it look like?'

'Round and made of glass.'

Prunella rolled her eyes. 'Can you be more specific?'

'It has snowstorms and flashes green and the imp has yellow eyes. He shows you the places he wants you to go.'

'The imp has yellow eyes you say?' said Prunella. She poured herself another cup of tea. 'And the snow globe flashes green? You have it here with you?'

Calypso shook her head again and waited for the next question she couldn't help but answer.

'Well, go and get this snow globe and bring it to my plane.' Prunella stood up and hooked her bag over her arm. 'And be quick, or else I'll send Featherlegs to collect it.'

'If I bring you the snow globe,' Calypso wiped a tear away, 'will you get Nova out?'

Prunella smiled. It wasn't a nice smile. 'We'll see.'

CHAPTER 17

Friends Again

Alfie headed for Mrs Mention's Tea Room.

What choice did he have but to trust the imp? After all, the imp had saved him from Shane Fagan.

As Alfie passed Blackstacks' Chemist's Shop, he saw a sign plastered across the door.

BY ORDER OF THE GOVERNMENT
OR WHATEVER
<u>CLOSED</u>
POISONOUS MEDICINES AND SO ON

The sign had been written in a spidery, angry-looking scrawl that didn't look official at all.

The blinds had been pulled down, but Alfie peeped through a crack and saw that, inside, the shop was a mess:

Bottles and packages pulled from the shelves. Powder dusted over the floor and pills spilled on the counter.

Who could have done this?

Alfie examined the sign, the spidery writing on it – *spidery* writing . . . Featherlegs, surely? The Head Witch must be behind this!

His poor aunts!

Their shop in ruins!

Zita in prison!

Gertrude alone!

The snow globe began to buzz in his pocket.

It was still showing Mrs Mention's Tea Room, only now it was flashing red. On, off, on, off – like a warning light.

'All right, all right.' Alfie headed to Mrs Mention's Tea Room.

★

Calypso sat all alone in the tea room. The Head Witch had waltzed out of the back door, leaving her in a daze.

Curious villagers were still trying to snoop in the front windows – furious that curtains should be drawn when there was a lovely celebrity to gawp at.

But it was just as well the curtains were drawn, what with Mrs Mention's customers all being plants.

Calypso shook her head. How could she have told Prunella all those things when she'd promised Alfie she'd keep them secret?

And now she had to get the snow globe and take it

169

to her evil aunt! If she didn't, Prunella would set Featherlegs on them.

Calypso wondered how all this had happened. She had never, ever snitched a secret before! But Calypso hadn't felt quite herself, had she? Then she remembered: the tiny ruby-red bottle, the bubble-gum-pink drops in her tea, the faint strawberry taste and the sudden urge to tell Prunella *everything*.

There was a faint rustling. All around the tea room the plants were becoming people again: twiggy branches were turning back into fingers and leaves into neatly curled hair. There was no sign of Mrs Mention among them, but, not wanting to be caught by her, Calypso searched quickly among the teacups. She found the bottle, empty now.

Engraved on the label, in elegant twisty writing, Calypso read:

TRUTH DROPS
Warning: May cause truthfulness
Pleasant bubble-gum flavour
Releases even the most stubbornly kept secrets

'Oh, the toad!' exclaimed Calypso. 'She gave me Truth Drops!'

Calypso pocketed the bottle and rushed to the door.

Alfie elbowed his way through a gaggle of villagers outside the front of the tea room. He was wondering how to get inside when the door opened.

It was Calypso.

'Run!' she cried.

★

They sat together in Calypso's bus.

Alfie looked at the ruby-red bottle in Calypso's hand.

'So, you see, Alfie, she gave me this potion so I'd tell her everything.'

Alfie nodded.

'I thought she was nice. I *wanted* her to be nice.'

'I know,' said Alfie quietly.

'You were right. She was tricking me all along,' Calypso said angrily, through her tears. 'Now I can totally believe that Prunella had something to do with Mum's disappearance.'

'I'm sorry.'

Calypso shrugged. 'And I'm sorry we fought.'

'A best friend is for ever,' Alfie replied. 'A fight won't change that.'

Calypso wiped her eyes and smiled.

Alfie thought for a moment. 'Do you think she'll free Nova if we give her the snow globe?'

'She'll probably just turn us into earwigs. She's a bully.'

'Nova is your sister. I think you should decide whether or not to give Prunella the snow globe.'

'I can't bear the thought of handing the snow globe over to Prunella. I feel certain she has some bad plan for it.' Calypso glanced at the door of the bus. 'But we can't just sit here and wait for Featherlegs to appear.'

Alfie felt full of fear again. He'd been trying not to imagine Featherlegs crawling over the bus and tapping on the windows. Pressing her face against the glass with that creepy sharp-toothed smile. And if there were really a row of extra eyes beneath her headband . . .

'I hate Prunella,' moaned Calypso. 'She's so desperate to be popular and yet she goes around turning people into plants and bugs and deceiving them into drinking Truth Drops. No wonder she's never been liked!'

For a moment Alfie almost felt sorry for Prunella. He had known that feeling in the playground whenever he had tried to make friends.

Before he'd met Calypso.

Calypso looked thoughtful. 'Why does Prunella want the snow globe so badly?'

'Maybe it's because the imp shows you stuff,' suggested Alfie. 'She could use it to keep an eye on her enemies?'

'Well, she's not having it!' Calypso's face clouded with worry. 'But what if she does send Featherlegs to take it?'

Alfie was trying not to think about that. 'I think we ought to hide the snow globe somewhere a lot safer than this rucksack.'

'You're right,' nodded Calypso. 'But where?'

Alfie thought for a moment, then said 'I know the perfect place.'

CHAPTER 18

Under the Library Ghost's Bonnet

In times of trouble: go to a library. If you need to lose yourself: find a library. If you are planning a difficult and dangerous adventure: a library is the place to do it. If you need to work out how to get yourself out of a fix, or into a fix: oh, you know where to go!

Don't go to a library if you want to throw books, talk loudly to yourself or eat hot dogs with drippy, gloopy ketchup. Gertrude was doing all of these things in the library at Switherbroom Hall. It was putting the ghostly librarian right out of sorts.

He greeted Alfie and Calypso at the door. 'A word, please, young people, if you will.'

The ghost led them to a pile of books taller than all of them.

'Gertrude is behaving even more strangely than usual,'

said the ghost. He pointed over the top of a pile of books. 'She's behind there.'

Calypso dragged a chair across (of the non-quarrelsome kind, luckily) and climbed up on it to see over the pile of books. 'She's *reading*!'

'This is a *library*, Calypso,' replied Alfie.

Calypso pulled a face.

Alfie climbed up on the chair too.

Gertrude, still in her dressing gown and slippers, was furiously leafing through a book. She had books to her left and books to her right: ancient books with leather bindings and yellowed pages. The books ruffled and snapped, like old bookish crocodiles. More books were pushing forward and stacking themselves up to be read.

Gertrude slammed the book on her lap closed and threw it on the pile to the right of her.

Rafferty, who was sleeping at her feet, opened one amber eye.

'She's looking for a spell to rescue Zita from prison,' the library ghost explained.

'Is that possible?' asked Calypso.

'Nope,' whispered the library ghost. 'Zita will be trapped in a witch bottle, of course; hidden somewhere you'd never think of looking.'

Gertrude let out a frustrated cry and threw a book across the room.

The ghostly librarian sailed forward. 'Madam, I would politely remind you to keep the noise down! The other readers!'

'What other readers?' scowled Gertrude. 'I don't see any other readers.'

'But that's not to say they're not there,' said the ghost huffily. 'Just because you can't *see* them.'

'Oh, keep your bonnet on! You ghosts are so touchy!' Gertrude squinted at the children. 'Are you hungry? What day is it?'

'We're fine,' said Alfie. 'Can we help at all?'

'It's all in Old Witch, a language even I don't understand. But thank you. And I hope you two are keeping out of mischief.'

Alfie glanced at Calypso. 'We're doing our best.'

'Fabulous,' said Gertrude, with her nose back in a book. 'Now, if you'll excuse me . . .'

She slammed the book shut with a cry of frustration and hurled it over her shoulder.

The ghost flinched.

The library ghost walked Alfie and Calypso to the door, or rather floated beside them as they walked to the door.

'You wouldn't happen to have a spell for dealing with a Head Witch for once and for all?' asked Alfie.

'Or a scary half-witch-half-spider?' added Calypso.

'Those would be valuable spells indeed,' smiled the library ghost. 'If they existed.'

Alfie took the snow globe from his anorak pocket and held it out to the library ghost. 'Could you keep this safe for us?'

'Not that imp again!' the ghost grumbled.

'Please,' said Alfie.

The ghost nodded and untied his bonnet ribbons.

He beckoned and the snow globe floated obediently from Alfie's hand and was gone.

'He's hidden it under his bonnet!' exclaimed Calypso.

The ghost tied his ribbons in a firm knot. 'That should do it: snow globes have minds of their own, don't you know?'

Alfie and Calypso were watching the visiting witches from Alfie's bedroom window. Somehow Alfie didn't mind Calypso seeing his room now. He knew she wouldn't judge him for the plastic joke fingers and Gertrude's spooky paintings on the wall.

The sound of excited shouts and cries drifted up from the lawn below where witches and their Familiars were competing in sack races, or five-a-side football, or a mysterious game which involved throwing angry-looking toads at each other and quickly running away.

The sports day had been organised in the Head Witch's honour, although Prunella was nowhere to be seen and neither was Featherlegs, thankfully. The door to the plane was closed and the steps were raised. The white trucks that had been arriving all afternoon were parked in a row outside Switherbroom Hall. Some of the guards stood around the plane with their arms folded. Others went snooping among the crowds of witches. They were dressed in white and wore smart white caps and tough expressions.

Calypso frowned. 'I don't like the look of those guards.'

'Me either, but the witches seem too busy with their games to notice them.'

Calypso's face brightened. 'Witches love contests, don't they?'

'It looks like it.'

'So, if we can't *pinch* the golden key from Prunella, maybe we could *win* it from her!' Calypso grinned. 'Prunella wants the snow globe and we want the key. So, we challenge her to a contest and if we win, she has to give us the golden key!'

Alfie thought a moment. 'But if we lose, won't we have to give her the snow globe?'

'We won't lose!'

'Why would she even agree?' asked Alfie.

'Well, we know from her diary that Prunella's always wanted to be popular, don't we?'

Alfie nodded.

'And she still wants to impress the other witches with her new hairstyles and trainers, doesn't she?' added Calypso.

'Seems so.'

'So, we tell Prunella that if she takes part in a contest it will make her popular with the witches. More than turning them into earwigs or whatever!'

Alfie watched the witches on the lawn below. The spectators were hopping, clapping, waving flags and generally having a brilliant time.

'She could just order Featherlegs to find the snow globe and then eat us,' said Alfie.

'Of course she could!' agreed Calypso. 'We have to make Prunella believe a contest would be even more fun than seeing us crunched up by that horror!'

It was a simple enough plan, but what sort of contest could they challenge the Head Witch to, and *most* importantly, how could they make sure that they beat her?

'I'm not sure we can beat her at anything,' said Alfie doubtfully. 'And even if we did win, what's to say she'd hand over the key?'

'It's the best plan we've got, Alfie.'

So, they found paper and pens and sat on Alfie's bed and tried to think of all the things they were good at.

Alfie nodded. 'You're good at the trapeze, but I can't think of one thing I'm good at.'

Calypso laughed. 'You're good at loads, Alfie! Reading books especially.'

'I can't imagine the Head Witch would want to do either of those.'

'You're right.'

'So, let's find out what she does like,' said Alfie. 'Wait, come to think of it, there's something in here that might help!'

Alfie picked up *Everyday Magic for Beginners*.

Calypso hid a smile.

Turning to a chapter titled 'Head Witches: Past, Present and Future', Alfie read aloud:

178

Prunella Formaldehyde Morrow: eldest daughter of Margot and Montague Morrow, granddaughter of Viola Morrow. Prunella has been the winner of the Best Witch Award in the 'Most Marvellous Spell' category for five years running. She is also the youngest Head Witch in history; taking over from Old Dame Riddle Blackstack was her 'absolute dream!' she says.

In her spare time, Prunella enjoys playing Snakes and Ladders with her Familiar. 'I always lose,' gushes Prunella, 'but I love it!'

'That's it!' Alfie tapped the page. 'We challenge Prunella to a game of Snakes and Ladders.'

'A game that depends on luck?' said Calypso.

'You can make luck.' Alfie smiled. 'There's a spell in here for it.'

'But what if we lose, Alfie?'

'We make it so we can't.'

Calypso's eyes widened. 'You mean we *cheat*?'

'I wouldn't *normally* cheat,' said Alfie, 'but it sounds like Prunella cheats all the time.'

'She's the biggest cheat of all!' Calypso said angrily. 'Let's do it, Alfie.'

CHAPTER 19

The Contest

Alfie and Calypso walked up to the aeroplane on the lawn outside Switherbroom Hall.

'We'll go to them before they come to us,' said Alfie bravely.

The witches had finished their sports day and were sitting around talking and drinking cups of tea. From time to time they glanced over at the guards or up at the plane. They nudged each other as they watched Alfie and Calypso approach, wondering if there could be a spot of trouble brewing.

Up close, the plane was huge and gleaming.

A guard in white uniform came forward, her face scowling under her white helmet. 'Business?' she barked.

'We're here to speak to the Head Witch,' said Alfie.

'She's expecting us,' added Calypso.

There was a scuttling noise above them. Featherlegs was creeping down the plane steps, all in black with her headband pulled low.

She smiled horribly at Alfie. '*Morsel*. Soft to eat.'

Alfie shuddered at the yellowing points of Featherlegs's teeth.

'Leave him alone,' said Calypso sharply. 'We're here to talk to Prunella.'

Featherlegs hissed and clambered back up the steps and into the plane.

'Ready?' Alfie asked.

Calypso nodded.

The walls of the plane were white, as was the floor. There were vases of snowy roses everywhere. Prunella sat on a fluffy white couch. She was wearing one of her floaty white dresses and a gloating expression.

She held out her hand. 'Snow globe.'

'Nope,' said Calypso.

Behind them Featherlegs hissed like a deflating balloon.

'Stop fooling about,' snapped Prunella. 'Hand over the snow globe or I'll let Featherlegs web you both up and bite your heads off.'

Alfie could feel his heart hammering in his ears. He took a deep breath. 'You can threaten us all you like, but we won't give you the snow globe.'

'Brave words, indeed!' Prunella laughed. 'You haven't seen what's under Featherlegs's headband!'

'Extra eyes. You don't scare us and neither does she,' said Calypso, doing her best not to sound scared.

Alfie glanced at his friend in admiration: she had such courage!

'So, why are you here, if it's not to bring me what I want?' asked Prunella.

'You have the golden key and we have the snow globe—' began Alfie.

'Get to the point, Blackstack.'

'We challenge you to a game, a contest. If you win, we hand over the snow globe; if we win—'

'Yeah, yeah,' said Prunella. 'I get it.'

'You're not very popular at the moment,' Calypso pointed out. 'No offence.'

Featherlegs started to untie her headband. Alfie noticed with alarm that the points of her yellow teeth were growing. They protruded from her mouth like sharpened knives.

'Lunch!' burbled Featherlegs.

'There's a way you could be more popular,' said Alfie quickly.

'Snack!' jabbered Featherlegs.

'Wait, Featherlegs.' Prunella held up her hand. 'Let me hear what they have to say first. Go on.'

'Witches love contests,' began Alfie.

'*Hello*.' Prunella looked bored. 'They've been holding events in my honour for days.'

'Yes, but you don't take part,' said Alfie. 'But if you did, it would show the other witches you are a good sport. They might even start to like you.'

'They've never liked me,' Prunella sniffed. 'What sort of challenge?'

'A game of Snakes and Ladders,' said Calypso.

Prunella's face brightened. 'I love Snakes and Ladders!' She thought for a moment. 'All right, I accept. But I get to choose where this contest is held.'

Alfie glanced at Calypso. She nodded.

'OK,' said Alfie.

'I choose . . .' Prunella pointed at Calypso. 'Your big top! We'll invite everyone. Your rag-tag circus people, all the villagers and all the witches.'

'Not the circus—' Calypso started.

'Yes, the circus, I want *everyone* to see I'm fun.'

Alfie frowned. 'But there can't be magic, I mean, if the villagers are there.'

'Why would I need magic?' sneered Prunella. 'I can easily beat a wimp like you and your nitwit friend there without using magic.'

'If you lose, you hand over the golden key,' said Alfie firmly.

'And if you lose, wimpy, you hand over the snow globe.'

The sun was setting, golden light spilling in through the bus windows. Calypso had found Alfie some pyjamas and a spare toothbrush. Gertrude was no doubt too busy to worry where he was.

They were cooking a meal for themselves on the hob

in the bus. Alfie waited for the water in the pan to start bubbling before he put the pasta in. This was the first normal thing he'd done in days!

'It's a good idea to stick together,' he said. 'I couldn't have gone to sleep up at the house thinking of Featherlegs creeping around.'

'Nor me.' Calypso had her nose stuck in a book. It was *Everyday Magic for Beginners*.

Alfie carefully added the pasta.

'Some of these spells look so difficult and they are just for beginner witches!' She glanced at Alfie. 'How do you feel about all this magic stuff?'

'It's a bit odd,' he admitted. 'But I'm sure we'll get used to it.'

'We're in it together at least,' said Calypso.

Alfie smiled into the pan. 'So, you don't mind me staying?'

'Of course not!' Calypso laughed. 'I haven't had a sleepover in ages.'

'I don't think I've *ever* had a sleepover. Only with Clarice when Dad was away. But she wasn't my best friend like you are.'

'Oh, Alfie, you really are so sweet!' said Calypso.

'Urgh, Alfie, you're *soooo sweet*!' said a voice at the door of the bus.

Shane Fagan stood in the doorway wearing his studded belt and black T-shirt. He pointed at Alfie. 'What's *he* doing here, Calypso?'

'Shut up, Shane! Leave him alone.' She paused. 'Have

you forgotten what happened last time you picked on him?'

Shane glanced nervously at Alfie. 'Weirdo,' he mouthed.

'What do you want, Shane?' asked Calypso.

'You're in trouble again.' Shane smirked. 'Granny Fagan wants to see you in her tent, *right now*.'

Calypso groaned.

Calypso and Alfie stood outside Granny Fagan's tent, next to a sign that said:

Park Your Hog Here

Calypso explained that a 'hog' is a large powerful motorbike. Granny Fagan liked nothing more than large powerful motorbikes. Which was why she always wore a leather jacket and trousers: they protected her arms and legs when she rode.

Granny Fagan's tent had a skull and crossbones flag flying from the top of it. The canvas was ancient and weather-stained. Some said it was as old as Granny Fagan herself, but no one really knew how old Granny Fagan was. There was a famous photograph taken on the opening night of Fagan's Family Circus, of a strongman holding a baby. The baby was supposed to be Granny Fagan, which would make her one hundred and fifty years old.

Granny's gruff voice called out, 'Calypso, get in here.'

'I'll wait outside,' whispered Alfie.

'Bring Alfie,' growled Granny Fagan. 'I know he's there with you.'

Alfie followed Calypso through the tent flap.

Granny Fagan sat in a chair smoking her pipe. The tent was very tidy inside. It had a camp bed, a table and a small stove. A lantern hung from the ceiling and there was a rug on the floor.

Granny Fagan squinted at them through the pipe smoke. 'You two have been busy.'

Calypso shrugged. Alfie coughed.

'Are you in need of having your fortune told, Alfie Blackstack?' asked Granny Fagan.

'Um,' said Alfie.

'Get the ball, Calypso.'

Calypso rummaged in a trunk beside the bed. She carefully carried a drawstring bag made of brightly coloured patchwork to Granny Fagan.

Granny Fagan put down her pipe and untied the bag. 'Take a seat.'

Calypso nudged Alfie and they sat next to each other on the rug.

Granny Fagan pulled out a round glass ball and set it on the camping table before her.

'A snow globe!' Alfie exclaimed.

Granny Fagan laughed. 'It's a crystal ball; it can show you the future.'

'It's magic then?'

'Sort of, but not the type you two have discovered.'

'How does it work?'

'I look into it, Alfie, then wait for the fog to clear.'

'Just like a snow globe,' said Alfie. 'Only snow globes have blizzards and not fog.'

Granny gazed into the crystal ball.

'What do you see? Is the fog clearing?'

'Nothing,' murmured Calypso. 'She makes it all up.'

Granny Fagan shot Calypso a stern look. 'The crystal ball says you ought to watch your mouth.'

Calypso grinned.

Granny Fagan turned to Alfie. 'You are braver than you think. You've not had an easy time, but I see better things ahead.'

Alfie hoped this meant Prunella Morrow wouldn't be turning him into an earwig.

Granny Fagan looked into her crystal ball. 'You have a great enemy, Alfie, but you also have a great friend.' She glanced at Calypso and smiled. 'You might win yet.'

'*Might* win?' cried Calypso.

'Nothing is certain if it hasn't happened,' said Granny Fagan. 'Win, lose – it depends on three things.'

'What three things?' asked Alfie.

'Head, heart and a little bit of luck . . . wait, there's an incoming message.'

Calypso rolled her eyes. 'It'll be "eat your vegetables and go to bed early".'

'Here comes the message.' Granny pointed to the tent flaps.

A bat shuffled into the tent.

The bat was battered and dusty – as if he'd flown in

from the other side of the world – but Alfie would have recognised Magnus anywhere.

Granny Fagan went outside to smoke her pipe, smoke not being good for children.

'Is Granny Fagan a witch too?' whispered Alfie.

'Never mind that,' Calypso said. 'The bat is trying to tell us something. Look, it's a mime.'

The bat was hopping and flapping.

'He has something stuck under his wing!' said Calypso.

The bat flinched but let Calypso pick him up. She gently unfastened a tiny black tube.

'It's like something you'd find on a cat's collar, Alfie!'

The bat looked indignant.

Along the side of the tube, in red letters, were the words:

FOR THE ATTENTION OF ANY
AVAILABLE BLACKSTACK

'It must be from Zita!' Alfie said, opening the tube. Inside was a curl of paper that he unrolled. 'It's a note, but it makes no sense, I don't understand . . .'

'There's an instruction there, Alfie, on the bottom line.' Calypso read it aloud:

This message is in code.
A kiss from a true Blackstack will unlock it.

'But it's been in a bat's armpit!' Alfie exclaimed.

Calypso gave Alfie a look.

'No offence,' said Alfie to the bat.

The bat wrinkled his nose.

Alfie kissed the note. The letters rearranged themselves.

WITCH IN DISTRESS

THIS BAT IS FITTED WITH A HOMING DEVICE.

In the unlikely event WITCH and FAMILIAR become SEPARATED,

please use the EYE-SPY spell to determine whereabouts of one

ZITALINA BLACKSTACK

(for spell, please turn over)

Alfie turned over the note. 'This spell has a recipe for a potion – it will take some mixing!'

'What about the snow globe and the contest?' groaned Calypso. 'Do we really have to save your grumpy aunt now as well as my little sister?'

CHAPTER 20

Eye-Spy

Night had fallen in Little Snoddington.

Imagine, if you can, the sleeping village lit by moonlight.

The tea room, empty now, with tables set neatly for the morning. In her bedroom above, Mrs Mention snored in her soft spongy bed under a strawberry-pink satin cover.

In the vicarage up the road, Mrs Vicar napped in her hard bed on her bumpy mattress, complaining about goats and underpants.

The peaceful church was fast asleep, the dust settled and still.

In the post office, all the stamps and letters slept, nicely stacked and folded.

The duck-pond ducks snoozed with their heads under their wings.

Only the owls were awake, and the foxes and the mice and all those creatures who begin their day when you and I go to bed.

And two children, they were awake too.

They crept across moonlit fields doing their best to keep out of sight of the plane on the lawn outside Switherbroom Hall and any guards (or children-eating half-spiders) that might be patrolling. They took the road through the dark forest to the village and ran through the empty streets to Blackstacks' Chemist's Shop.

Alfie still had the key in his anorak pocket from the time he was supposed to mind the place. He opened the front door and they crunched across broken glass to Zita's mixing room. Alfie found the light switches and Calypso put the bat down on the counter.

Magnus was looking worse by the minute.

'Poor thing,' said Calypso with pity. She kissed the fluffy mouse hair on his head very gently.

Magnus gnashed his fangs weakly; he seemed exhausted from the ordeal of getting to them.

Alfie and Calypso searched among the rubble for something they could use to revive a magical bat. Alfie found a small purple bottle. It looked very old. He read the faded label:

FROGGE RESTORATIVE
FORE WEBBY FEET AND MOISTE EYES IN
YOUR FAMILIAR
10 DROPS ON A FLYE AT BEDTIME

'Could this work?'

'Ask the bat,' said Calypso.

The bat squinted at the label and shrugged.

There were no flies, but Alfie found a raisin in the biscuit tin under the counter. The bat took his medicine and a few moments later coughed into action. He stretched his wings and hobbled to the edge of the counter. Then he sneezed. Then he gazed towards the window with watery eyes.

'He wants to get back to Zita,' said Alfie.

'Then let's start the spell and find her.'

Alfie read aloud from the note retrieved from the bat's armpit. The ingredients for the spell were as follows:

A large jar of powdered cloud

Two fresh hare ears

One plump eyeball

A handful of dragons' teeth

Unicorn droppings

Nutmeg to taste

The children looked around Zita's mixing room, reading the labels on jars and packets.

'Dragons' teeth!' Alfie held up a box of sharp green teeth.

Calypso found a jar of fluffy white cloud and a packet of something that looked like wizened banana peel. 'Guess what this is!'

Alfie grimaced. 'Unicorn poo?'

'But where are we going to find fresh hare ears and an eyeball?' asked Calypso. 'There's no way I'm going to hurt an animal. Not even to help your grumpy aunt.'

Alfie nodded. 'I agree.'

Then on the top shelf he spotted them.

EVIL EYE GOBSTOPPERS

'We'll use one of those sweets for an eyeball!' he said.

The gobstoppers were large and bloodshot. They stared out of the jar. Alfie selected a large dark brown eyeball with a big black pupil.

'What about the hare ears, Alfie?'

'That plant in the corner has leaves a bit like ears, long and sort of pointed.'

Calypso looked doubtful.

'Let's just give it a go,' said Alfie.

They lit the camping stove they found in a cupboard. It burned with a green flame and had the words WITCH GAZZ on the side. Then together they lifted a heavy cauldron to rest on top of it.

Calypso carefully opened the jar of cloud. It looked like meringue and came with a small net attached to the lid of the jar in case the cloud drifted away.

Calypso shook the cloud into the cauldron. It landed with a soft PLUMPH.

Alfie threw in the gobstopper and the long pointy leaves.

There was some nutmeg powder on the windowsill; they shook that in with the unicorn poo and dragons' teeth.

'I'll stir,' said Alfie. 'You say the spell.'

Calypso held up the note.

A witch lost, a Familiar found, is no way to proceed,
So, here's a special finding spell for a time of need.
Eye and ears join as one to fly into the sky,
To see and hear our witch in trouble and help her by and by!

Alfie and Calypso waited.

Green flames danced under the cauldron.

Calypso peeped inside. 'The cloud looks like a dishcloth. I can't see the gobstopper – maybe it's melted?'

Alfie looked again at the note. 'It says to put a lid on.'

They put a lid on the cauldron. And waited.

Magnus tapped a clawed foot and stared out of the window. The sky was brightening; it would be dawn soon.

Alfie turned over the note. 'We missed a bit; there's some more to do.'

Calypso took the note and read:

While the potion is bubbling you will need to find:

a mirror
a conch shell
a turnip

They found a mirror under the counter, a seashell in a drawer and a bunch of radishes by the coat rack.

Alfie held up a radish. 'This will have to do: it's a vegetable, isn't it?'

'I'll say the next part of the spell,' said Calypso.

Mirror, mirror on the wall,
Who is the magic-ist of all?
Three times tapped with my turnip-end,
Now show me the witch who needs a friend!

Alfie tapped the mirror with the radish. 'Done. Next the shell.'

Calypso read aloud again.

Shell so pearly, shell so white,
Plucked from a sunny beach.
Let me hear the poor lost witch,
Who's somewhere out of reach!

A sudden popping noise came from inside the cauldron.

If you've ever made popcorn, you'll know the sound that kernels make when they start hopping and bursting and fluffing up.

This was the same sort of sound.

Alfie gingerly removed the lid. And out flew something quite remarkable.

The Eye-Spy flew a loop around the room, flapping its long leafy ears. The eye in the centre turned here and there; the pupil had changed from brown to green now and the white of the eye was even more bloodshot. It looked like a real eyeball and not like a gobstopper any more.

'Alfie, it worked!' laughed Calypso, ducking. 'It's a bit terrifying though.'

The Eye-Spy shot towards the window.

'Alfie – it wants to get out!'

Alfie threw open the window and the eye was gone.

Magnus fluttered wonkily to the edge of the workbench, then flew after it.

'What next, Alfie?' asked Calypso, her head out the window. The Eye-Spy and the battered bat were just specks in the sky now.

'I suppose we wait for that thing to find Zita.'

The message in the mirror said:

WATCH THIS SPACE . . .

Otherwise the mirror was fogged and greenish in colour.

Alfie drew a crumpled sheet of paper from his anorak pocket. 'While we're waiting, we could make these?'

'What are they?'

196

'Just a few spells I copied out of Zita's book.' He glanced at the shreds that littered the floor. 'Before Featherlegs destroyed it.'

'You want to make more?' Calypso groaned. 'We've been working on spells all night!'

'Just take a look.'

ENEMY MINIMISER
Shrink your favourite enemy to the size of a bug
No known side effects, other than making things
very, very small

'We could shrink Featherlegs back to her proper size,' suggested Alfie.

'Good thinking!' exclaimed Calypso.

They worked together to make the potion, stirring until the gloopy mixture turned into sparkling blue powder.

'Do you think Shane would mind if we tested it on him?' said Alfie with a smile.

Calypso laughed. She checked the mirror. It was still fogged, showing the words:

WATCH THIS SPACE . . .

'Do you think it will take long?' said Calypso. 'We ought to get back before everyone wakes up, and we've the contest to get ready for!'

The shell on the workbench began to ring. Words were flashing on the surface of the mirror.

INCOMING
WITCH LOCATED
WITCH-NAV ACTIVATED

'The Eye-Spy has found her!' exclaimed Alfie.

They held the shell up between them so they could both listen. Together they peered into the mirror to see what the Eye-Spy saw.

'It's flying so high!' said Calypso. 'Look at the tiny houses and cars!'

Alfie could see that – it made him feel a bit sick to see the rooftops and treetops, but he kept watching the mirror.

He saw a familiar building.

'It's London! That's the Natural History Museum, where my dad used to take me.' He pulled a face. 'To look at mouldy old birds' eggs.'

'I've never been there – I'd love to take a closer look!'

As if in answer, the Eye-Spy swooped low and plummeted down the side of the building.

It was almost more than Alfie could stand. But then up, up into the sky again the magical flying gobstopper went, over . . .

'Tower Bridge!' shouted Calypso.

'The Houses of Parliament!' laughed Alfie.

Then the mirror fogged and more words flashed up.

WITCH INSIDE . . .
HIGH-SECURITY PRISON

'It doesn't look like a prison,' said Calypso.

She was right. What they saw in the mirror looked nothing like a prison!

They were seeing . . . wait for it – an allotment!

The Eye-Spy flew low over runner beans and tomato plants until it reached a rickety shed. An old man with a large and drooping moustache and a stout stick in his hand was snoozing on a deckchair outside.

A weasel was curled up at his feet.

Neither of them noticed a flying gobstopper eyeball and bedraggled bat flop in through the half-open door of the shed.

CHAPTER 21

The All-Purpose Get-Out-of-Jail Spell

Alfie glanced at Calypso. She was holding her breath and staring into the mirror.

The Eye-Spy was rolling along a shelf in the shed in the allotment; all they could see was a dusty jumble of seed packets and garden twine. Then a row of glass jars, each with a screw top.

But wait! In each jar . . . there was a person!

Tiny WITCHES!

The tiny witches were banging on the glass and shouting. But Alfie and Calypso couldn't hear a word they were saying.

In the last jar was Zita.

Zita wasn't banging on the glass or shouting. She was sitting cross-legged with her head in her hands. She looked defeated. The Eye-Spy tapped on the jar. Zita startled and jumped to her feet. She began to say something.

'We can't hear through the jar!' Alfie called.

The Eye-Spy hopped nearer, sticking itself to the glass.

Zita's face appeared, large and surprised in the mirror, her voice muffled like she was underwater. 'Gertrude, is that you?'

'It's Alfie,' said Alfie loudly, into the shell.

'Where's Gertrude?'

'She's trying to find a spell to get you out!' shouted Calypso.

'No need to shout,' sniffed Zita. 'Look in my spell book: the All-Purpose Get-Out-Of-Jail Spell.'

'Featherlegs ripped up your spell book,' said Alfie.

'And wrecked the shop,' added Calypso.

'I'LL FLATTEN THAT BUG!' cried Zita. She glanced around and lowered her voice. 'Prunella is still at Switherbroom Hall?'

'Parked in her plane outside,' replied Alfie.

Zita bit her lip. 'Don't let Prunella get inside the library, whatever you do!'

'What is it that she wants from there?' asked Alfie.

'Granny Morrow – we keep her in the library. During the last Witch War, she was turned into a chair.'

'Prunella wrote about Granny Morrow in her diary!' said Calypso. 'She's always dreamed of changing her back.'

Zita looked puzzled. 'You've read Prunella's diary?'

'It's in the library at Switherbroom Hall.'

'Goodness,' said Zita. 'There's a rumour that Prunella

has found a way to reverse the Forever Spell – the spell used on Granny Morrow in the first place.'

A thought struck Alfie. 'What does Granny Morrow look like?'

'Twisty legs, green leather, likes to skulk in corners,' answered Zita.

'I've sat on Granny Morrow!' exclaimed Alfie.

Calypso frowned at him.

'Sorry,' said Alfie.

'If Prunella succeeds, we're done for! No one could beat her with Granny Morrow at her side!' Zita paced the jar. 'You two must help me escape.'

'What can we do?'

'I have some All-Purpose Witching Powder hidden in the toe of my sock, Alfie. The guards didn't notice it. I'll make up a new spell and if you both say it with me, it might just work!'

I suppose you'd like to know the spell you need to say to get out of witch prison (if you ever find yourself shrunk to the size of a plum and trapped in a jar in an allotment shed).

Here's the spell that Alfie and Calypso and Zita said together:

Head Witch, it isn't fair to keep us all here
* caught.*
With this spell we're breaking free – this ain't the
* jail you thought.*

Lids unscrew, glass walls shatter – prison is no
  more.
Raise your voices, magic friends, to an angry roar!
Witches near and far, say this good spell-rhyme.
We're busting out, right here, right now, because
  it's FREEDOM TIME!

They waited.

Zita stood very still inside the jar.

Magnus stared sorrowfully through the glass at his poor witch, who was so much smaller than him for a change!

Alfie and Calypso sat watching it all in the mirror.

There was a flash of green and the mirror went foggy.

'KEEP PRUNELLA OUT OF THE LIBRARY; I'M ON MY WAY!' boomed Zita's voice from the shell. 'WE ARE AT WAR!'

CHAPTER 22

Morrow's Family Circus

Alfie and Calypso stood at the entrance of the big top. There was still the small matter of a Snakes and Ladders competition with the Head Witch. Alfie and Calypso didn't say so, but they knew it was even more important to get that key and open the globe and save Nova. Once Zita arrived, all manner of trouble would start. Witches would be turning each other into sticks, zooming through the sky, making green flashes. Or at least that's what Alfie thought might happen in a Witch War.

Calypso told him that she'd smuggle him out with the circus.

'I don't want to leave you behind,' Calypso had said. 'I couldn't bear it if you were turned into a chair.'

Alfie hadn't known quite what to say.

*

The big top was hopping.

Tom Fagan was in the centre of the ring, directing the circus folk who were running everywhere. Lights were being tested in dazzling, flashing, spinning patterns. Carpenters were adjusting the bandstand and setting out more benches. But Alfie thought it felt very different to the last time they were there. There was no Nova for a start. And no one smiled now.

High above Alfie and Calypso's heads a web of ropes and narrow walkways was taking shape. They looked up at it with great puzzlement.

'Wait!' Alfie cried. 'I know what it is! It's a Snakes and Ladders board. Only it's not laid out flat on the ground!'

The walkways ran behind white wooden squares, which each had a number attached. There were sparkly gold-painted ladders to climb up and long green rubbery snakes to slide down.

The board stretched up to the ceiling of the big top. There were *hundreds* of squares!

'It's so high,' said Calypso.

Alfie shuddered; he had a bad feeling about this. 'We can't win, Calypso. Look what she's building.'

'It's only a few ropes and rubbery snakes, Alfie.'

'Now it is, but what if Prunella starts using magic?'

Calypso couldn't answer him, because at that moment Tom Fagan was walking over.

'Cal, Alfie, stay clear while we're setting up. This television celebrity wants all sorts of crazy stuff.' He glanced around. 'Is Nova with you?'

'She's safely tucked away.' Calypso quickly changed the subject. 'What crazy stuff does the celebrity want, Dad?'

'She wants us to flood the ring with water and take away the safety nets.' He shook his head. 'I won't do either. It would be far too dangerous.'

'I told you!' Alfie whispered. 'Prunella wants to finish us off!'

'Shh,' said Calypso.

'The money she has offered will cover the whole run at Little Snoddington,' Tom carried on. 'After all, we didn't sell any tickets for our own show.'

'Thanks to Mrs Mention!' muttered Calypso.

'Mrs Mention is supporting this event though,' said Tom bitterly. 'She couldn't be happier that a celebrity is hosting a game show in Little Snoddington!'

A huge sign was pulled up. White letters on a black glittery background read:

MORROW'S FAMILY CIRCUS
THE FIRST, THE LAST, THE BEST!

Calypso scowled at the sign. 'She's changed the name!'

'She's bought our circus for the day,' said Tom, 'so she can do whatever she wants.'

★

It had been a dreary old morning up at Switherbroom Hall. There were only so many races the witches could run and card games they could play and cups of tea they could drink. And they disliked Prunella's guards – always snooping about and barking orders and searching everyone's cauldrons for spells against the Head Witch. Nothing fun or eventful seemed to be happening now.

The visiting witches had started to talk about going back to their homes when suddenly Prunella's helicopters took to the sky, one by one, with a whirr of their blades.

Once they were hovering overhead, the helicopter doors opened and green confetti tumbled down.

A shout went up. The confetti was made of tickets!

The witches elbowed each other out of the way to grab the tickets as they fell, or pluck them from bushes, or scoop them up from the ground.

'There's trouble afoot, Moley!' said Hester Bodkin as she watched the helicopters buzz off over the chimneys of Switherbroom Hall.

Moley O'Malley sniffed and the droplet that often hovered on the end of her nose shook but didn't fall. 'Hester, that way London lies.'

Her Familiar, the fat toad perched on her shoulder, stuck out his long tongue and tasted the air. He gave a farty croak.

'Brian says Zita has escaped.'

Hester put her hand in the pocket of her black dress, drawing out a scraggy rat and holding it up to her ear. 'Steven says he might be right.'

Moley picked her teeth with a long fingernail. 'Of course, London would be the place to hide a witch prison. Big place, tiny bottle.'

A green ticket blew past and got stuck on the point of Moley's witch's hat.

Hester picked it off and read the words out loud:

AN INVITATION TO MORROW'S
FAMILY CIRCUS
THE BIGGEST CONTEST EVER!
SNAKES AND LADDERS
THE HEAD WITCH WILL PLAY AGAINST
MYSTERY CONTESTANTS
PRUNELLA IS FUN AND FAIR!

'Ooh,' said Hester with delight. 'Here comes a juicy bit of trouble!'

'What's the Head Witch up to?' whispered Moley.

'What's Zita Blackstack up to?' Hester whispered back.

All around them witches were unpacking cats and cauldrons.

Everyone had decided to stay, of course.

Gertrude had her ticket too. Rafferty had brought one into the library where she slept snoring in her chair, surrounded by books.

Rafferty jumped lightly on her lap and purred into her ear.

But she slept on.

The library ghost was busy herding the books from Gertrude's huge pile back to their shelves. The books were bad tempered. They hissed and snapped their covers at the ghost.

Now and again he stopped to glance at the gnarly legged chair. The chair seemed to be watching him.

'Hold your tongue, Granny Morrow,' the ghost said to the chair. 'Or I'll have you chopped up for firewood! Just let Prunella try to change you back!'

The chair growled and slid into a corner.

The library ghost loosened his bonnet and scratched his ghostly head – if only Zita were here!

But Zita was nearer than he knew.

Beyond the village, on the other side of a hill, Zita was trying to sleep under a hedge at the side of the road.

She was grubby and tired, as anyone kept in a jar in a potting shed would be. But she was not alone. She had an army. A gaggle of witches Zita had helped to escape from the witch prison. Shelf after shelf of trapped witches – all of them Prunella's enemies. And they had found more witches as they escaped through the allotment. Witches held captive in greenhouses! Witches jailed in watering cans!

Now Zita and her rag-tag army were on their way to Switherbroom Hall with armfuls of spells and hearts full of courage. They just needed a few ingredients and a cauldron or two. Maybe a few fast vacuum cleaners. They would arrest Prunella Morrow for all the horrible things she'd done and throw *her* into prison.

Somehow.

They weren't quite sure how.

No one had ever arrested a Head Witch before.

CHAPTER 23

Snakes and Ladders
and Crocodiles

By mid-morning, the sun was high and the day was hot. The crowds were arriving. There were kiosks for candy-floss and toffee apples and cold drinks. Clowns ran about pretending to throw buckets of water over everyone. The circus band played happy tunes.

The audience began to form two queues, one either side of the entrance to the big top.

On the right, the villagers of Little Snoddington stood holding blue tickets.

These tickets had been found posted through letter-boxes or propped on mantelpieces, stuck on car windshields or just fluttering down the main street.

Mrs Mention stood at the front of the blue queue. She had closed the tea room and given herself a day off.

Everyone in *this* queue tried not to stare at the people in the *other* queue.

The people in the left-hand queue all seemed a little *odd*.

They held green tickets. Some wore rainbow leggings and bright tops, others wore shapeless dresses in black. A few of them wore tweed suits.

Several were holding toads or snakes, or had rats perched on their shoulders. Several more had weasels standing nicely by their ankles like well-trained dogs.

But really most of the Familiars had their own entrance around the back (so as not to alarm the villagers). They slithered and climbed, wiggled and flew into seats behind the bandstand.

For the show was about to begin!

Calypso and Alfie sat backstage in a dressing room filled with white roses, mirrors and a plump white couch. Two guards in white uniforms stood at the door.

Alfie was wishing himself back in his old life in London, which was wonderfully free from adventures.

London was a dream now.

Witches were real.

He glanced at Calypso sitting next to him in her denim shorts, with her grubby knees and her messy ponytail. She was biting her nails and glancing around the room.

She caught Alfie watching her and smiled.

He smiled back.

He might have to live the rest of his life as an insect. But he had a friend, a *best* friend.

That alone was magic.

From the sound of reluctant clapping outside they could tell that Prunella had arrived.

She swept into the dressing room with Featherlegs in tow.

'Ready to lose, piglets?' said Prunella with a sneer.

Prunella was wearing the most ridiculous outfit. She looked like one of Mrs Mention's meringues, in layers of white taffeta studded with sparkling crystals, and on her feet she wore pointy high-heeled shoes.

'These are the rules,' she said. 'One of you throws the dice, the other climbs along the board. The first team to get to the final square will win.' She smiled. 'But watch out for the snakes!'

Calypso frowned. 'How are you even going to climb in that outfit?'

'Oh, I'm not climbing. I've a sore finger.' Prunella held up a perfectly healthy-looking finger. 'Featherlegs will do the climbing.'

'That's not fair!' exclaimed Calypso. 'She's half spider!'

'Let's ask the judge.' Prunella turned to the door. 'Will you hurry up, Lady Frogmore?'

A very ancient witch wobbled in.

Lady Frogmore was wearing a monocle around her neck. She held it up to her eye and peered at Alfie.

'Open your mouth, say "ahhhh".'

Alfie opened his mouth. 'Ahhhh.'

'Good,' nodded Lady Frogmore. 'What's your favourite food?'

'Crisps,' Alfie answered.

'Excellent,' said Lady Frogmore. 'Mine too.'

She opened a leather case and pulled out an instrument not unlike a stethoscope. She held one end of it to Alfie's forehead and listened carefully. 'Thoughts whirring nicely in there, Blackstack.'

'How long will this take?' Prunella huffed. 'I've a contest to win.'

Lady Frogmore turned to Calypso.

'Don't bother examining her,' said Prunella rudely. 'She's a Morrow.'

'So she is.' Lady Frogmore rummaged in her case again and pulled out a fat paper scroll.

Prunella looked to the heavens.

'Here are the rules and regulations of the Witch's Challenge,' said Lady Frogmore. 'Witches must agree to abide by these before they play for any prize.' She glanced at Prunella. 'Because some witches are sneaky.'

'Oh, give it here!' Prunella grabbed the paper. 'Where do I sign?'

Lady Frogmore cleared her throat. 'I must now remind you of the rules and regulations of the Witch's Challenge.'

Prunella stamped her foot. 'We'll be here all day!'

Lady Frogmore ignored her.

In case you are wondering, these were the rules Lady Frogmore read out:

Rule One: No good-luck magic

Rule Two: No magic for the purposes of sabotaging your opponent

Rule Three: No using magic to give yourself brilliant skills

Rule Four: All other magic is probably all right

Rule Five: In the case of injury during the game, the other side will nominate a replacement and a change of dice may be requested

Rule Six: Failure to hand over prize to the winning contestant will result in . . .

A BIG OLD FINE

MAYBE PRISON

Lady Frogmore turned to Calypso and Alfie. 'You are playing to win Prunella Morrow's golden key?'

Prunella dangled the golden key on her necklace with a mocking smile.

'Yes,' said Alfie.

Lady Frogmore turned to Prunella. 'You are playing to win the snow globe currently belonging to Alfie Blackstack?'

'Yep.'

When the scroll was signed, Lady Frogmore closed it in her leather case. 'Then let the contest commence!'

★

Calypso kicked off her trainers, pulled her ponytail tighter and stood at the entrance to the ring of the big top. She had insisted on climbing. They both knew they stood a better chance with Calypso on the ropes and walkways. Alfie felt relieved for himself but scared for Calypso!

Featherlegs took off her shoes and her cloak. Alfie and Calypso watched in horror as first another set of arms, and then, second, another set of legs folded out from under the Familiar's cape. Featherlegs stretched and waggled each thin bare foot and each long-fingered hand in turn. The nails on her four feet were purple and sharp. The nails on her four hands were green and pointed. Featherlegs reached up and untied her headband.

'I can't look!' exclaimed Alfie.

Calypso gasped.

Alfie looked.

The headband was off. And there, on the Familiar's forehead, was a line of huge ink-black insect eyes. Some blinking and some staring, all of them glittering with spite. Featherlegs grinned, revealing her knife-like set of yellow teeth, and dropped down onto her hands and feet. She scuttled off, stopping to turn her head right round to look behind her with her evil spider-eyes.

'Looosssers,' she hissed.

Alfie and Calypso walked out to the sound of clapping and cheering and the band playing. They stood in the middle of the ring, not knowing what to do. Alfie searched the audience for a friendly face and found one. Granny

Fagan. Wearing a leather jacket with skulls on it. She nodded at Alfie and he felt a little better.

Featherlegs scurried out.

The band stopped playing.

There were a few cries of fright from the audience. A small child in the front row started to scream.

Prunella swept into the ring. She had changed her outfit. Now she was wearing silver spangled tights and a white tailcoat and top hat.

She was the ringmaster!

'LADIES AND GENTLEMEN, BOYS AND GIRLS!' she beamed. 'WELCOME TO MORROW'S FAMILY CIRCUS!'

The small child in the front row screamed louder.

Prunella strolled forward. 'Can't you shut that thing up?'

'She's not a *thing* and that creature is scaring her!' The child's granny pointed at Featherlegs, who blew a loud raspberry.

The other villagers bum-shuffled in their chairs. A few of them muttered something about it not being right to scare children at the circus.

'Will you all ZIP IT?' said Prunella rudely. 'You're ruining my show.'

Another audience member stood up. 'Celebrity or no celebrity, we haven't paid good money to be spoken to like this!'

'Hear, hear,' said the villagers. 'Even if you are off the telly!'

'Oh, shut up, you dimwits!' cried Prunella.

With that, several members of the audience stood up to leave.

'SIT DOWN,' roared Prunella, startling the child in the front row, who began to scream even louder.

'BE QUIET!' Prunella pulled a silver bottle from the pocket of her tailcoat, blew a handful of green powder over the front row and said something under her breath.

The audience gasped.

The screaming child was now a small shrub rose.

Her mother screamed – POP! – she became a bush!

One after another the villagers were transformed into potted plants before they could open their mouths, or make a run for it, or even blink!

The witches knew better. They kept to their seats and stayed very still.

Alfie stood horrified, frozen to the spot. Until his eyes met Granny Fagan's.

Granny Fagan sat among a forest of green. She was the only audience member on the village side who wasn't a plant. Even the circus musicians were plants now.

Alfie was wondering why Granny Fagan wasn't a plant when a guard grabbed him by the arm. (If he had spotted Mrs Mention slip out of the big top with not a leaf in sight, he might have asked the same of her.)

The guard marched Alfie up to a cross marked on the floor, next to the Snakes and Ladders board. Alfie looked up at the board. It was a web of glitter and rope and wooden walkways.

'Let's press on!' said Prunella. 'May I present the world's

most perilous and thrilling game of Snakes and Ladders!'

The witches in the audience clapped, trying to ignore the rows of potted plants across from them.

'The snakes are slippery and the ladders are rickety!' continued Prunella cheerily. 'There are no nets or safety harnesses because I removed them!'

She laughed merrily and pointed up to the ceiling of the big top. 'We will go up very, very high! And could fall down very, very far!' Then she stamped. 'SPLAT!'

The audience of witches jumped.

The audience of potted plants trembled a bit.

Featherlegs had already climbed halfway up the board and was hanging from a rope by her teeth.

Alfie looked at Calypso. She stood in her bare feet at the bottom of the board. She glanced back at him and managed a nervous smile.

'Do you like your Snakes and Ladders *dangerous*, witches?' Prunella sang.

The witches were dumbstruck. They hardly knew how to answer.

'THE ANSWER IS "*YES*" FOR GOODNESS' SAKE!' roared Prunella.

'YES!' chorused the witches.

'SO DO I!' shouted Prunella. 'Which is why *I* like to add . . .' She tapped the ground with her whip and the floor of the big top melted away. 'CROCODILES!'

Alfie looked down in amazement. Calypso, Prunella and himself now stood on three white platforms rising from a ring full of swampy water.

219

In the swampy water, huge long crocodiles turned and thrashed.

'AND WHAT'S MORE, MY CROCODILES ARE STARVING!' bellowed Prunella. 'AREN'T YOU, BOYS?'

As if on cue, the crocodiles rose to the surface of the water and snapped at the air.

A cry rippled through the audience. The witches craned their necks to see.

'Now let me introduce our contestants!' continued the Head Witch. 'Playing for Team MORROW, we have FEATHERLEGS, a really top-notch Familiar!'

A few witches forgot themselves and booed.

Prunella looked around flintily. 'Featherlegs is on the GOOD team!'

The witches cheered unenthusiastically.

'Playing for the other lot, we have Calypso. She has nits and is untrustworthy.'

The witches sent up a loud 'Boo'.

Prunella nodded approvingly.

'Lady Isadora Frogmore will be keeping an eye on the proceedings to make sure they are . . .' Prunella smirked, 'fair.'

Lady Frogmore tottered to her seat at the side of the ring, squinting through her monocle. Alfie heard the voices of the witches sitting in the audience behind him.

'I can't imagine anything about this game will be fair.'

'Featherlegs will mince those kids!'

'They'll be wrapped in a web in no time.'

'With their heads bitten off!'

'And their brains slurped up!'

Alfie tried to concentrate. He repeated what Granny Fagan had told him: *head, heart and a little bit of luck*.

With a little bit of luck, Zita would arrive soon.

'Joining Lady Frogmore is our guest of honour, Gertrude Blackstack.'

Alfie watched in dismay as Prunella's guards marched Aunt Gertrude into the ring. They pushed her to a seat and threw a wriggling bag at her.

Gertrude let Rafferty out of the bag. The pair of them sat blinking and scowling.

'This will be Gertrude Blackstack's last day at Switherbroom Hall,' said Prunella triumphantly. 'She's decided to take a very long trip. A nice cruise perhaps.'

Gertrude's eyes met Alfie's. She frowned and shook her head.

'I shall be staying on at Switherbroom Hall,' crowed Prunella. 'I'll take good care of the place for the Blackstack girls!'

The witches behind Alfie began whispering again.

'Take care of it my foot. Prunella has stolen their house!'

'She wants what's in the library!'

'What's in the library?'

'Hester Bodkin, you are the stupidest witch ever! Granny Morrow – the chair!'

'And you, Moley O'Malley, are a toad-faced know-it-all. What use is a chair to Prunella?'

'She's found a way to change Granny back – from chair to witch!'

'Undo a Forever Spell? That's not possible, Moley!'

'Yes, Hester, it is apparently, if you are the Head Witch.'

'Bats alive! Granny Morrow was properly wicked. No one would be able to win against *her*.'

Other voiced joined in:

'The Blackstacks are done for!'

'What will the Head Witch do with Gertrude?'

'Throw her in jail with Zita!'

'What of that boy, the nephew?'

'Spider snack.'

'Or turned into a pebble, or maybe a stick?'

'An earwig – that's her current favourite.'

Head, heart and a little bit of luck, Alfie thought to himself.

Prunella, on her platform, clicked her fingers. A dice fell into her hand. 'I play first, because this is *my* circus, after all.'

A table appeared before her. Prunella rolled the dice.

'A five!' she exclaimed. 'That takes us – oh, yes! To the foot of a lovely long ladder!'

Featherlegs swung to the square marked 5. Then she ran up a sparkling golden ladder to square 147. There she hung off the rope and made rude gestures with all four hands.

Prunella chuckled. 'Your turn, Alfie Blackstack,' she said, and threw the dice across the swampy water.

Alfie (to his surprise) caught the dice.

A table appeared in front of him. He took a deep breath and threw a 3. He looked up at the board anxiously: just a regular square, no ladder.

'Go on then,' said Prunella to Calypso. 'Hop to it, nit girl.'

There was a big stretch of swampy crocodile-infested water between Calypso's platform and the Snakes and Ladders board.

'How do I get across?' Calypso asked.

Prunella laughed. 'You're a circus monkey. Should be easy enough. Strike up the band while we wait for this nitwit to play her move!'

There was silence.

'I SAID MUSIC!' Prunella roared.

A few witches stepped forward and moved aside the potted plants that used to be the circus musicians. They took up the instruments and began to play a rackety tune.

Calypso turned to Alfie, her face terrified. 'What should I do?'

There was no way to swim across. Alfie, shuddering with fear, watched the crocodiles thrash and snap.

If only Calypso could walk on water!

Then he noticed something – there was a pattern to the movements of the crocodiles: they were following the tune the witches were playing!

Sometimes the crocodiles surfaced, smirking, sometimes they turned and sometimes they swished. They had a routine, like synchronised swimmers!

'Calypso,' he said. 'The crocodiles have a dance routine. You have to time it right.'

Calypso looked too, then she smiled and nodded. She waited for the crocs to line up, just before they started to dive and swish. She took a deep breath . . . and ran for it!

The crocodiles were as surprised as the watching witches. A few crocs snapped at Calypso's ankles as she sprang from back to back. The witches clapped and stamped in delight as Calypso made it to the board and swung along to square 3.

Prunella turned to the audience with a snarl. 'You'd better cheer the *right* team or you'll end up as potted plants too!'

The witches stopped applauding.

'Better,' barked Prunella. 'Now that our contestants have got the hang of it, let's speed it up.' She beckoned the dice. It flew from Alfie's table into her hand. 'My turn!'

Alfie could hardly keep up.

The dice rolled, Featherlegs and Calypso ran and jumped from square to square and the audience watched, on the edge of their seats. Prunella strutted up and down her platform, laughing when Calypso stumbled on the ropes, scowling when Calypso stopped herself falling into the open grins of the crocodiles.

Everyone was far too busy following the game to notice the guards moving around the outside of the big top, closing all the exits.

Granny Fagan, however, did notice.

She slipped along the aisle, under the bandstand and out through the assorted Familiars. Her crystal ball had shown her that much more than a bat was approaching.

Calypso looked near to tears. Her hands were burned from the ropes and she had grazes all over her legs and arms. Featherlegs could run at an incredible pace and there were hundreds of squares to cover.

The snakes were the worst though.

They were made from slippery rubbery foam. Each time Calypso slid down them – and she seemed to be getting more than her fair share of snakes – her hands and feet lost contact with the board for a few alarming moments. Alfie could barely watch.

Featherlegs was miles above Calypso; she'd had ladders all the way and not one snake.

Alfie took a deep breath. It was their turn again next. He prayed for a ladder, or at least not another snake. He suspected that Prunella had put a spell on the dice. Nothing seemed fair about this game! Lady Frogmore was hardly a good referee: she was fast asleep with her mouth open.

Alfie threw a two – hooray, a ladder! But when he looked again the number had changed – it was a five!

'Five!' cried Prunella. 'Oh look, a big long snake!'

'You changed it!' shouted Alfie. 'I threw a two!'

'Nonsense,' laughed the Head Witch. 'You're just a bad LOSER!'

Alfie glared at her. He had a jar of Enemy Minimiser Powder in his anorak pocket, but the Head Witch was too far away for him to use it. How he wished he could shrink Prunella and then squash her like a bug! Her and Featherlegs both!

They were losing. Calypso was exhausted, stumbling and slipping.

What were they thinking? They had known nothing about magic until a few days ago – why had they challenged the most powerful witch of all?

CHAPTER 24

Alfie's Trial

Something was afoot in the big top. The witches in the audience were whispering together and nudging one another. The word was that Zita had broken out of prison and raised an army. She was on her way to fight Prunella Morrow.

The witches had had enough of the Head Witch's entertainment. There she was gloating and teasing those two poor kiddies. And there was Featherlegs, scampering and smirking and licking her chops. And then what about all the villagers sitting in their pots, trembling and leafy? And, even worse, Prunella's guards, standing at the exits with their arms folded and their faces steely.

Enough was enough!

The witches in the audience, young and ancient, good-ish and bad-ish, vowed to fight on Zita's side.

If she ever arrived . . .

*

Alfie looked up from the dice.

It was the worst possible throw.

It landed Calypso at the mouth of the biggest snake yet. It would send her right back to the start! There would be no way they could win now. The audience knew it too; they sat in gloomy silence.

Featherlegs hung above Calypso's square, her glittering eyes on the tired girl. The Familiar's mouth drooled.

'That spider's going to pounce!' blurted one witch.

'That kid's in trouble!' spluttered another.

But Alfie didn't notice. He stood shaking his head, his eyes to the ground, the dice in his hand with the losing throw on it.

Featherlegs dropped down with her fangs bared.

'Watch out, Calypso!' cried one witch.

'Look up, Calypso!' shouted another.

Everything happened very quickly.

Featherlegs closed in.

Calypso pulled out a jar and sprinkled sparkly blue powder on her hand.

A spell! The audience held their breath.

But Featherlegs was too quick for Calypso and sank her teeth into the girl's wrist.

Calypso screamed, stumbled and fell – she was heading towards the crocodile-crawling water!

Alfie's heart stopped.

The audience jumped to their feet.

'Foul play!' shouted the witches. 'That spider bit her!'

'SHUT UP,' Prunella roared. 'SIT DOWN.'

But where was Calypso? Could the crocodiles really have eaten her that quickly?

The witches looked into the murky swamp water. The crocodiles bobbed and grinned.

Then Alfie saw his friend, hanging by her ankle from a rope halfway down the board.

Alfie and Calypso stood on the platform together. Calypso leant on Alfie's shoulder, her foot too painful to put on the ground, her ankle already swelling.

'A substitute for Calypso must be found,' Lady Frogmore declared.

'I can play!' insisted Calypso.

'According to the rules,' said Lady Frogmore, 'you must pick her replacement, Prunella.'

'But that's not fair! Featherlegs bit me!' Calypso held up her wrist to show a line of red bite marks.

'Him.' Prunella pointed at Alfie. 'Wimpy boy, but I doubt he'll even get past the crocodiles.'

'You can do this, Alfie,' said Calypso. 'You're one of the bravest people I know!'

But Alfie didn't feel brave.

'You talk to a ghost, for heaven's sake, in a haunted library!'

Alfie laughed and held out his shaking hands. 'I'm like a jelly!'

Calypso laughed too. 'All right, so no climbing in our next adventure.'

'"Our next adventure" – do you think we'll have another one?'

'We'd better, Alfie!' said Calypso.

Alfie stood on his platform. Between him and the Snakes and Ladders board lay a stretch of swampy water. Containing crocodiles. He looked at Calypso. She was standing ready with the dice. She gave him a worried smile.

He looked out into the audience. He couldn't see Granny Fagan, but the witches in the audience looked back at him with sympathy. Like the crocodiles, the witches knew he was going to fail.

Then all of a sudden Alfie realised something.

He may not be quick or strong or brave, but he had a job to do. More than this – he had a friend who *believed* he could do it. So he was going to try.

'I'd like some music,' said Alfie.

'Oh, just get on with it,' groaned Prunella.

Alfie turned to Lady Frogmore. 'And a new dice. That's allowed, isn't it, with a change of player? It said so on the paper I signed.'

Lady Frogmore nodded. 'It certainly is, Master Blackstack! Here's someone who reads the small print!'

'Alfie reads everything,' said Calypso.

'No!' shrieked Prunella. 'I won't have it!'

'You signed the rules too, Prunella,' Lady Frogmore pointed out. 'Anyone would think you've put a spell on the dice.'

A chuckle went through the audience.

Prunella turned red.

'Music and a new dice, please.' Lady Frogmore smiled. 'Ready, Alfie?'

Alfie watched the crocodiles and listened to the music.

Rumpeta, rumpeta, rumpeta.

But then he heard something else.

Outside there was shouting and, above the big top, a droning vacuuming sound. Alfie had heard a sound like that before – when the witches arrived for Prunella's party.

A guard ran on stage and whispered something to Prunella. Her face fell. She looked annoyed.

She turned to Alfie. 'If you're playing, play! I haven't got all day!' she snapped.

Alfie looked up. Featherlegs was almost at the finish line and he wasn't even on the board! What was the point in trying?

Well . . . there was a whacking great snake between Featherlegs and the finish line. With a dice that Prunella hadn't put a spell on, they might just stand a chance, if Alfie could get past the crocodiles . . .

The shouts outside were getting louder and so were the sounds of the vacuum cleaners. Now there were bangs, pops and whizzes, too!

Rumpeta, rumpeta, rumpeta.

The crocodiles danced. He had to time it exactly right.

With his eyes on the dancing crocodiles, Alfie didn't see the witches slyly searching under hats or in bags and pockets for little silver bottles of green powder and unstoppering the bottles ready. Neither did Alfie see the guards drawing forward with their own supply of green powder.

Rumpeta, rumpeta, rumpeta.

Alfie jumped.

Calypso had made it look easy. Alfie slipped on the last crocodile but managed to grab the rope. He hung on for dear life.

It was the worst and the best thing he'd ever done!

The audience were on their feet, clapping and hollering.

Alfie waved at them.

Prunella, scowling, threw the dice.

A three for a snake, a six for the finish line.

It was a six!

Featherlegs danced along the board gleefully.

Prunella clapped and laughed. The crocodiles vanished. A burst of glitter overhead.

Alfie slowly climbed down, tested the ground to make sure it was solid and went to join Calypso.

'I won!' gloated Prunella. 'I won!'

All was lost.

It was at that very moment, with a wild, high battle cry, Zita and a troop of witches poured in through every door of the big top.

Alfie was astounded.

Zita Blackstack looked transformed.

She strode through the audience, tall and queenly in her black leather battledress and cape. Her raven-black hair was pulled tightly back. Around her waist she wore a belt studded with silver bottles. She held a shield decorated with a raven in one hand. In the other hand, she grasped the neck of a shiny black vacuum cleaner. Its nozzle whipped from side to side like the head of an angry snake. Over her head swooped Magnus the bat, his eyes burning fierce red.

Alfie had to admit: Aunt Zita looked cool.

Behind her marched assorted witches.

'Prunella Morrow, you are under arrest,' said Zita, her voice clear and stern. 'You are the worst Head Witch the world has ever seen.'

Gertrude jumped to her feet in delight.

The audience whistled and hooted.

'Codswallop.' Prunella took a little silver bottle from her pocket.

Zita rushed forward.

Several guards stepped up to meet Zita.

Clouds of green powder exploded in the air.

Prunella grabbed Alfie by the hood of his anorak. 'Come any closer and the boy's an earwig!'

Zita glanced at Alfie. Then she gestured for the other witches to step back. 'Don't you dare harm my nephew!' said Zita fiercely.

Alfie, in the grasp of the worst Head Witch the world had ever seen, felt joyous.

Aunt Zita was standing up for him! He was her *nephew*! It *mattered* to Zita that he wasn't an earwig!

'Hand over the snow globe, you,' Prunella snarled at Alfie, tightening her grip on his hood.

Lady Frogmore woke up and struggled to her feet. 'May I remind you, Alfie, that you agreed to hand over the snow globe if you lost the challenge.'

'Hurry up!' demanded Prunella, giving Alfie a shake. 'I want my prize! Where is it?'

'It's at Switherbroom Hall,' admitted Alfie. 'Under the library ghost's bonnet.'

'The library?' said Prunella. 'That's just where I'm heading!'

Featherlegs flew a large white vacuum cleaner into the ring. She hovered next to Prunella.

'If you think I'm bad, wait until you meet my Granny Morrow!' Prunella yelled as she jumped on the back of the vacuum.

Featherlegs grinned. Prunella and her Familiar took off and flew out of the door in a flash.

The witches looked at Zita.

'Let's get after them!' she shouted.

The witches cheered.

'DOWN WITH THE HEAD WITCH!'

'DOWN WITH PRUNELLA!'

There was a great rumbling roar outside the tent.

The witches stopped cheering.

Granny Fagan rode into the ring on her hog. She revved the engine; it was the noisiest thing Alfie had ever heard in his life. He noticed with surprise that Granny Fagan also wore a belt with silver bottles on it. Her own supply of All-Purpose Witching Powder!

Granny Fagan pushed the visor of her helmet back. 'Alfie, Calypso,' she called. 'Jump on!'

CHAPTER 25

Cracking the Library Code

Granny Fagan's motorbike roared through the streets of Little Snoddington and came to a screeching halt outside Blackstacks' Chemist's Shop. The village was completely empty – the villagers were still potted plants in the big top!

Alfie and Calypso jumped off the motorbike. Alfie's legs were still a bit shaky from the bumpy, terrifying, terrific ride! They handed their helmets back to Granny Fagan.

In the distance, somewhere over the circus Alfie imagined, there were loud bangs and fizzles. The whole sky lit up with flashes of green light.

It sounded like the most humungous firework display Alfie could imagine.

He glanced at Granny Fagan. 'Will my aunts be all right?'

'Let's just worry about finding supplies. Your aunts will be here soon.'

'Will they be able to fight off the guards, Granny?' asked Calypso. 'Shouldn't we go back and help?'

'We are helping: we've potions to collect.'

There was a sudden clank and a whirr.

Even Granny Fagan jumped.

Everyone looked around.

Two white tanks, each with the sign of the dove painted on its side, came rolling down the village street. The first bumped up on the pavement and squashed a postbox. The second rolled over a parked car, flattening it like a crisp packet.

Suddenly, in the sky above the tanks, two blurred shapes appeared, accompanied by the drone of vacuum cleaners.

Zita and Gertrude!

Zita, bent in close to her machine, spun through the air. Magnus shot alongside like the sharpest of darts.

Gertrude, wearing swimming goggles, bounced along on her vacuum with Rafferty in a shopping basket tied on the back.

The tank turned its turret – it was taking aim at Alfie's aunts!

Zita swooped low and a cloud of green powder erupted. When the cloud cleared, Alfie could see that the tank was now made of cardboard. The guards kicked their way out in disgust, waving their fists at the flying witches.

'Go on! Let them have it!' shouted Granny Fagan. 'Tanks in Little Snoddington, who would have thought it?!'

Calypso hopped inside Blackstacks' Chemist's Shop, leaning on Alfie's arm and wincing at the pain in her ankle. Alfie found a stool and helped her to sit down. Gertrude said a quick spell and wrapped Calypso's ankle in a bandage soaked in something green and slimy. Almost immediately Calypso could move without too much pain.

Zita had stalked through the shop into her mixing room, closing the door behind her. She hardly seemed to notice the mess Featherlegs had made.

Witches began to arrive at the shop in dribs and drabs. Some held sticks and stones and one, an egg whisk. These witches had tears in their eyes, because the objects were once their friends.

Soon the shop was full to bursting with witches, all talking at once.

The door to Zita's mixing room opened. She pointed at Alfie and Calypso.

'You two, in here.'

Zita was holding the note that Alfie had found stuck to the door.

'I think it was written by Featherlegs, with the spidery writing,' he ventured.

Zita nodded. 'On Prunella's orders, of course.'

'I'm sorry about your shop.'

Zita shrugged. 'Let's deal with Prunella; we'll worry

about the shop after. We might stand a chance if we can get to the library before she cracks the code and gets inside.'

'What code?' asked Alfie.

'The library door is protected by a secret code and is impossible to open, even with magic. It's also very clever: if a stranger tries to go into the library, the door slams shut and locks itself.' She paused. 'On account of all the rare or deadly things inside.'

'Like Granny Morrow?'

Zita nodded. 'Like Granny Morrow.'

'The library door didn't shut me out when I first arrived.'

'Because you weren't a stranger, Alfie,' said Zita. 'It knew right away that you belonged at Switherbroom Hall.'

Alfie smiled and, to his surprise, Zita smiled back.

'What about the snow globe?' Calypso reminded them. 'That's in the library too. Prunella mustn't get her hands on it!'

'Snow globe?' said Zita. 'What snow globe?'

'Mr Fingerhut gave it to me,' admitted Alfie.

'Describe it.'

'Round and glass with an imp in it,' Calypso ventured.

Zita looked like she'd won the lottery. 'Tell me about the imp!'

Her eyes widened as she listened to Alfie's description. 'I do believe that's Wormfrall, king of the imps!'

'Is that good?' replied Alfie.

'King Wormfrall disappeared when Mrs Mention cut

down his tree,' explained Zita. 'Of course Prunella was involved – she'd always hated the forest for some reason.'

Calypso gasped. 'Remember that photograph the imp showed us on Mrs Mention's mantelpiece, Alfie?'

'Sort of.'

'The celebrity in the white dress, standing next to Mrs Mention . . .'

'It was Prunella!' realised Alfie.

'Prunella had no business poking her nose into village business.' Zita looked cross. 'Her and Mrs Mention are as thick as thieves!'

'Prunella wanted us to bring her the snow globe,' said Alfie.

'Of course she did,' replied Zita. 'She trapped Wormfrall in that globe – she wouldn't want her angry enemy released.'

'Just as well we hid it then!' exclaimed Calypso.

Zita looked thoughtful. 'If we could just set Wormfrall free . . .'

'And Nova too!' cried Calypso.

Zita frowned. 'Nova? I don't under—'

'ALL HANDS ON DECK!' Gertrude came bursting through the door. 'Grab what you can and follow. Prunella has broken into Switherbroom Hall! We must defend the library!'

CHAPTER 26

The Invasion of
Switherbroom Hall

Switherbroom Hall was in a sorry state.

The front door had been blasted off and the chimneys had toppled down. The windows were broken and there was a hole the size of a moon crater where the front path used to be.

Granny Fagan, with Alfie and Calypso on the back, steered her hog past the hole and drove around the side of the house.

There was no sign of Prunella or Featherlegs but the plane was still there. It had been pelted with eggs. The words 'PRUNE IS A MAGGOT' had been painted on the side.

There was no sign of the Head Witch's guards either. A tank the size of a shoebox stood on the veranda surrounded by pebbles. The helicopters now seemed to be made of something soft, white and fluffy. They were sinking lopsidedly into the lawn.

Alfie and Calypso climbed off the motorbike and handed Granny Fagan their helmets. Calypso was only limping a little now; Gertrude's first aid had worked like magic.

Zita flew down on her vacuum and landed on the lawn. Gertrude and a flock of witches on vacuums bobbed through the sky close behind.

Other witches were arriving by way of bicycles and a bus borrowed from Little Snoddington Primary School. A touch of magic had turned the bus green and given it fairy lights and curtains and a refreshment bar. (Witches like to travel in style whenever they can.) Some of the Familiars sat on the witches' laps, pressing their noses to the bus windows as they looked out. The bat and bird Familiars flew above.

And so the witches gathered. Alfie and Calypso among them.

Zita held up her hand and everyone fell quiet. 'Prunella must be somewhere inside the house.'

'There's no one to be seen!'

'Where are all the guards?'

'This looks like a trap!'

Alfie could hear murmuring behind him. A witch with a frizz of silver hair was talking to the scraggy rat on her shoulder. They were inspecting the abandoned helicopter.

The witch stuck out her tongue and licked it.

The rat jumped off her shoulder and sank into the cockpit.

Alfie could hear excited squeaking.

'It's marshmallow!' the witch exclaimed. 'Here, Moley, try it!'

Another witch turned around. Alfie recognised her: it was the witch who had offered her toad to him for a cuddle. 'Hester, shut your trap; Zita's about to talk!'

Zita had climbed up on a garden table. 'Will those with *flying* Familiars stand next to Granny Fagan? You'll search the grounds.'

A number of witches shuffled over to Granny Fagan.

'Will those with Familiars with *sharp teeth* stand next to Gertrude? You'll go in through the front of the house and take the upstairs.'

Moley O'Malley joined Gertrude's team. Soon the group was ringed with dogs and foxes, ferrets and mice.

She took out her toad and whispered to him, 'Brian, keep your mouth closed. I know you've no teeth, but this is the best team for not being turned into a stick.'

The toad blinked. He wasn't impressed.

'Will those with Familiars who are *sly and silent* stand next to me? We'll go in the back way and head to the library.'

A witch put her hand up. 'Begging your pardon, Zita, but my Familiar is both sneaky and sharp of tooth, being a snake.'

Another witch put her hand up. 'My Familiar can't fly, has bad teeth and farts quite loudly, so he won't be good on the sly. Which group should we join?'

'Just join the group you think is best.' Zita looked around. 'All right, is everybody ready?'

The witches held up their weapons – mostly silver bottles, every pocket bulged with these. One witch waved a garden rake and others carried tennis racquets and saucepans. They all gnashed their teeth and looked equally ferocious whether they wore rainbow smocks and leggings, or dreary black dresses, or beards and tweed suits.

'If you see a fellow witch fall,' said Zita, 'pick them up. We may be able to change them back some day.'

Several witches, their faces upset and angry, held up various small objects.

'Ready?' asked Zita.

The witches nodded grimly.

'Then witches . . . good luck!'

Alfie and Calypso waved goodbye to Granny Fagan, who saluted as she roared off on her hog with her troop of witches following. A flock of far-sighted Familiars flew above.

Then they waved goodbye to Gertrude, who rushed off round the house with her troop. Rafferty joined the pack of tooth and clawed Familiars (cats and dogs working together just for the day).

Alfie and Calypso followed Zita and her witches in through the back door.

The Familiars, mostly snakes and weasels, went rushing off to scout out the ground floor. A group of fierce-looking witches armed with cans of Magical Bug Spray volunteered to search the corners of every room to see if they could catch Featherlegs. Another group would keep watch by the back door in case any guards showed up.

Zita set off across the hall with Alfie and Calypso following. 'Stay close to me, you two.'

Halfway down the hallway Alfie realised that everything was not quite right. The tiles were moving under his feet.

Then Calypso cried out. Alfie looked round; his friend was ankle-deep in the hall floor!

'Shh!' said Zita. 'Keep your voice down and don't move. Prunella has cast a Quicksand Spell.'

Alfie tried to get a foot free, but he was stuck too. It was the oddest sensation! The marble floor had turned to something like soup. Stone-cold soup! Stone-cold soup that was sucking him in!

'I don't like it!' said Calypso. She struggled and sank to her knees. She gave a shriek.

'Don't move, I said!' hissed Zita. 'The more you struggle, the more you'll sink. Just give me a minute and I'll make a counter-spell.'

'What's a counter-spell?' Calypso whispered to Alfie.

'A spell to reverse the first spell – in this case to turn quicksand back into stone.'

Zita searched through the bottles in her pockets. Alfie noticed that she was careful to stand on the edge of the patterned floor, on a spot that was still solid stone.

'I've got it!' Zita sprinkled green powder on her hand from a silver bottle and blue powder from a golden bottle.

She mixed them with her finger and blew the blend over the children while rhyming a spell.

Would you like to know what spell to say if you are ever stuck in magical quicksand?

> *Sand-be-slow and sand-be-quick – this isn't*
> *   playing fair,*
> *Leave go the children sinking deep on every*
> *   marble square.*
> *Hear these words I say to you, O soupy killer*
> *   floor,*
> *Make stone not sludge underfoot, yes, how it was*
> *   before!*

There was a green flash and a sucking noise. First Calypso bobbed up and then Alfie. They stood barefoot on cold marble tiles.

'My trainers!' moaned Calypso. 'The floor has eaten them! They were my best pair.'

'You're lucky not to have been swallowed up, Calypso!' snapped Zita. 'Now, keep the noise down, watch where you're stepping and follow me. We'll use a shortcut to the library.'

Zita tapped the wall and a hidden door creaked open.

'A secret passage!' exclaimed Alfie.

Zita ducked in through the doorway. 'Follow me!'

It was dark in the secret passage. Zita struck a match. It burned brightly with a steady green flame. She held it up before her, and Alfie could see that the walls were damp and mouldy and the ceiling was low. The floor felt gritty under his bare feet. The passage sometimes sloped up or down, often very steeply. From time to time Zita opened a spy-hole in the wall and peeked through. Next to each spy-hole was a label. Alfie caught glimpses of them as they rushed past:

BALLROOM
BROOM ROOM
POSH PARLOUR
CAULDRON CUPBOARD
HAUNTED GUEST ROOM

The secret passage wasn't a nice place to be. It smelt of mice and in some places was very full of cobwebs. A bit *too* full of cobwebs.

Alfie heard a scuttle behind him. He thought he saw a line of glittering eyes.

'Aunt Zita,' said Alfie. 'I'm not sure about this passage.'

Zita stopped to look at a label attached to a spy-hole. It read:

BATS' ATTIC

'That doesn't make sense.'

'What doesn't make sense?' asked Calypso.

'We're much lower down than the attic.' Zita sniffed. 'Somewhere near the kitchen; it smells mousier there.'

Alfie heard a clicking noise, like the sound of many sharp nails tapping the passage floor. 'I think something is following us, Aunt Zita.'

But Aunt Zita wasn't listening. 'This label is new; someone has been meddling!'

Alfie turned, listened and walked back a few steps – into a wall of cobwebs!

You know that feeling, don't you? When you walk through a cobweb you haven't seen? Fine and drifty and sticky! You brush and brush it away. If you're unlucky, you'll get a spider in your ear. If you're very unlucky, she'll set up home there and have a family and all you'll hear are spidery footsteps as they go about their business.

If you're very, *very* unlucky, like Alfie was, the web will belong to a child-eating witch's Familiar.

CRASH! Alfie was pulled over.

FRIZZZZZZZ! Alfie was spun up tight in a cocoon of super-sticky web.

DRAAAG, BUMP! Alfie was pulled headlong down the secret passageway.

BANG! His head slammed into a corner.

BASH! His knees whacked against a wall.

SWISH! He slid along the floor.

POP! He was pulled through a door in the secret passageway.

PLOP! He landed on the floor in a hallway.

Alfie looked up. There was the library door. And there was Prunella Morrow.

CHAPTER 27

Spider Webs and Spaghetti

Calypso and Zita tried to chase after Alfie down the secret passage, but it was no use – the thick cobwebs slowed them down!

What's more, the exits had all been boarded up.

'We're like mice in a maze!' said Zita.

'What about Alfie?' cried Calypso. 'Featherlegs will eat him!'

'Prunella will use Alfie to get into the library, *then* Featherlegs will eat him,' corrected Zita. 'Wait, I need some time to think.'

They stood still in the corridor.

'Now Alfie has gone as well as Nova!' Calypso fought back her tears. 'I'm never going to get them back.'

'Nova has gone where?' asked Zita.

'The imp imprisoned her in the snow globe. That's why we were trying to get Prunella's golden key.'

'What for?'

'To let out the imp so that he would free Nova! We tried to pinch the key from Prunella and when that didn't work we had to challenge her to that crazy game of Snakes and Ladders to win it.'

'You tried to *pinch* the golden key from the Head Witch? You and Alfie?' Zita looked impressed. 'The most powerful witch in the world?'

Calypso shrugged.

'It's true that you'd need the golden key to release the imp,' said Zita. 'But the imp couldn't have trapped Nova in the snow globe.'

'I don't understand,' said Calypso.

'Nova must have put herself in there,' explained Zita. 'Perhaps she sensed trouble was coming!'

'No way!' Calypso shook her head. 'The imp captured Nova; he said so!'

Zita smiled. 'King Wormfrall, if it is indeed him, is a bit of a joker!'

Calypso thought a moment. 'So we don't need the golden key to release Nova?'

'No,' said Zita quite kindly. 'You just need to tell your sister to stop being a little imp and come out!'

Calypso groaned. 'We needn't have challenged the Head Witch!'

Zita laughed. 'On the contrary, you showed the witches

that it's possible to stand up to a bully! You were both very brave.'

Calypso smiled.

'Right,' announced Zita, fishing in her pockets. 'I have a plan.'

She extracted a bedraggled gobstopper in the shape of an eyeball and two crumpled leaves.

'The Eye-Spy!' exclaimed Calypso.

'We can still help Alfie, even if we can't find a way out of this mouse maze.'

Prunella cleared cobwebs from Alfie's face.

'Urgh! Icky!' She wiped the web on the wall.

Featherlegs crouched nearby making disgusting slurping noises.

'Quiet, Featherlegs!' snapped Prunella. 'I know you're hungry, but you'll have to wait!'

Alfie was trussed up so tightly he could hardly breathe. This stuff was a million times stronger than an ordinary spider's web; it was like being wrapped in super-sticky silk thread.

'Now, Blackstack, open this door,' demanded Prunella. She tapped the door with one pink fingernail.

It was definitely the library door, because it had a painted sign saying LIBRARY on it, but today it looked different.

It was bristling with locks and peppered with keyholes.

'I don't know how,' said Alfie. 'It wasn't locked before.'

'You, boy, are entirely useless!' Prunella tried the handle, but the door was shut and locked fast. She fiddled with a few of the locks. Then she stamped her foot and kicked the door.

'OPEN UP!' she shouted. 'By order of the Head Witch!'

A ghostly face pushed through the locked door and frowned at Prunella. 'Who is knocking at my door?'

'He is,' said Prunella, pointing to Alfie slumped on the floor. 'Alfie Blackstack.'

The library ghost sniffed. 'That's as may be, but the library is closed today.'

'Toad warts it is: the sign says "Open".' Prunella pointed to a sign hung over the door handle that read 'Open'.

The sign quickly flipped over to 'Closed'.

'If your name is Morrow,' said the ghost. 'The library is most definitely closed.'

Prunella spoke bad words under her breath. Then she smiled at the ghost. 'I can stay outside. Just let the boy in.'

The ghost glanced at Alfie, then pursed his lips. 'Let me consider.' He closed his eyes.

Prunella waited, tapping her foot.

Featherlegs waited, licking her lips.

The ghost opened his eyes. 'How do I know that's Alfie Blackstack you have out there?'

Prunella went red. 'Would I lie?'

'Yes.'

251

Prunella kicked the door again.

The librarian held up a ghostly hand. 'I will ask the young man three questions. If he can answer any of them correctly, *proving* he is Alfie Blackstack, I shall open the door.'

'Don't open the door!' cried Alfie. 'She wants to turn that old chair back into Granny Morrow!'

'Shut it, you!' hissed Prunella. 'Fire away. But you have to open the door if he gets an answer right.'

'Agreed. First question,' said the ghost to Alfie. 'What was the filling in the sandwich in your suitcase the day you arrived in Little Snoddington?'

Prunella nudged Alfie with her foot.

'Jam,' said Alfie.

'Wrong!' said the ghost. 'Fish-paste. Next question: what animal did Shane Fagan try to make you kiss?'

'A goat,' said Alfie.

'Wrong! It was a horse, of course!' said the ghost. 'Final question coming up . . .'

Prunella bent close to Alfie. 'You'd better get the next question right, kiddo,' she hissed. 'Or else.'

'I'm not scared of you,' said Alfie, who was very scared of her indeed.

Prunella beckoned Featherlegs over. The spider scrambled up to Alfie.

'You think you've seen all her teeth,' Prunella nodded to her Familiar. 'But you haven't. Not the *special ones* that she'll use to crunch a hole in your head.'

Featherlegs grinned.

252

'Show him your skull-drilling teeth. Close up now. So that he can get a proper view.'

Featherlegs came closer . . .

'Closer still, Featherlegs, don't be shy!'

Featherlegs came closer still . . .

Alfie could feel the Familiar's breath on his cheek. She smelt revolting. Of rotten things dug up!

Featherlegs grinned wider. Then she opened her mouth and two long fangs sharper than steak knives slid into place.

'Bone crunch!' she burbled. 'Salty brain!'

Alfie screwed up his eyes. He didn't want to see any more!

A drop of drool from Featherlegs's mouth landed on his cheek. He felt her sharp teeth on his scalp.

'Now get on with it, ghost,' demanded Prunella. 'Ask him the last question.'

'Last question, Alfie. What object did you turn Rafferty the cat into?'

'A butter dish,' said Alfie miserably.

'Correct!' nodded the ghost.

Prunella tried the door handle. The door was still firmly shut.

'The boy answered correctly,' Prunella fumed. 'NOW OPEN UP, GHOST!'

'Hold your horses. I have to issue Master Blackstack with a library card first. It may take a little while.' The ghost winked at Alfie.

Prunella began to hop.

*

Alfie tried not to listen to the slurpings and hissings, the burbling and burpings of Featherlegs as she stood guarding her meal.

Alfie closed his eyes.

He could still smell her mouldy breath.

'Tassssty boy,' Featherlegs hissed. 'Good treat.'

Alfie listened instead to Prunella arguing with the library ghost.

It sounded as if the ghost was enjoying himself.

He hoped Calypso was all right and Gertrude and Granny Fagan and . . . OK . . . Zita too.

Someone *would* come soon!

Someone *had* to come soon!

In the meantime, Alfie would try to think happy thoughts. To take his mind off the fact that he was about to be a spider's meal.

He thought of making pasta in Calypso's bus.

Of laughing together as they cast their first spells.

Of Calypso bravely standing up to Shane for him.

Featherlegs poked him with her sharp green fingernails. 'Plenty eat!'

Alfie took a deep breath. He would shrink this spider if it were the last thing he did.

Granny Fagan rode her hog at full tilt.

She wasn't called a daredevil for nothing.

The grounds around Switherbroom Hall were clear of Prunella's guards, but some witches in white uniforms had been seen creeping off in the direction of the village.

Granny Fagan gave chase!

Her bike roared through fields and jumped over ditches, hurtled through alleyways and spun over bridges.

Hester Bodkin (Granny's second-in-command) kept up on her vacuum as best she could. She didn't have a flying Familiar, but her rat, Steven, could go fast if she threw him (although Steven objected strongly to this).

Their gang of witches was right behind them, on vacuums, scooters, bicycles and one on roller skates (their transport had a dash of magic – you could tell by their speed and their glowing green wheels).

Little Snoddington was empty. Perhaps the guards were hiding!

Granny Fagan made everyone park behind the church. Then they all crept back to the high street.

Just in time to see a villager.

The *only* villager not to be sitting in the big top in a pot, sprouting leaves.

Not only was Mrs Mention *not* a potted plant, but she was riding down the high street *on a vacuum cleaner*.

She landed outside the tea room and went inside.

Hester nudged Granny Fagan. 'If I'm not mistaken—'

'Mrs Mention is a witch,' finished the old daredevil.

Granny and Hester were looking with great interest at Mrs Mention's big white vacuum cleaner parked on the pavement outside the tea room.

'It's top of the range,' said Hester. 'With that button on it: "Turbo Magic Injection".'

'Air hog,' murmured Granny Fagan admiringly.

It had the sign of the dove on the side.

'It looks like someone might just be a pal of the Head Witch,' growled Granny Fagan.

The witches crept into the tea room. From Mrs Mention's kitchen came a baking smell – delicious and doughy and gingerbready.

And flashes of green light.

Granny Fagan pushed open the door so they could peep inside.

Mrs Mention stood with a cookie cutter in one hand and a bottle of All-Purpose Witching Powder in the other. There was dough and flour everywhere.

'She's making a gingerbread army!' Hester whispered. 'Look at the wee biscuit people!'

'Look at their wee sharp teeth!' said Granny Fagan.

As if in answer, Hester's Familiar gnashed his. Steven the rat thought this army smelled good enough to eat.

The gingerbread soldiers stood side by side in a line, each a foot tall.

The kitchen door creaked.

A gingerbread soldier looked around. 'Intruders!' it shouted in a sticky sort of voice.

'ATTACK!' shouted the gingerbread army, and rushed towards the door. Currant eyes gleaming!

Granny Fagan grabbed a broom. Hester grabbed a chair. Steven bared his teeth.

*

Gertrude and her troop of witches sneaked in through the front door as Zita had told them to.

There was not a guard to be seen.

In the hallway, Gertrude tapped the head of the snake banister. Its eyes glowed red. Gertrude bent her ear to the snake's head and listened carefully.

A plump witch with a toothless toad on her shoulder, Gertrude's second-in-command, nudged her.

'What does the house say?' asked Moley O'Malley.

Gertrude held her finger to her lips and continued listening. Then she motioned to the witches to draw nearer.

'There are guards all over the house,' reported Gertrude, keeping her voice low. 'Some have disguised themselves as lamps and occasional tables. Some are just hiding under the beds and behind the curtains.'

'Waiting to jump out and surprise us!' one of the witches softly replied.

'Not a very nice surprise!' mumbled another.

'Let's get 'em!'

'Turn them into sticks!'

'Stones!'

'Cat poo!'

The witches gave a hushed cheer and waved their bottles of All-Purpose Witching Powder.

'Best of luck, witches!' said Gertrude. 'Are you ready? On my count: one, two, THREE!'

Alfie, a neatly web-wrapped parcel on the hall floor, lay with his eyes screwed shut listening to Prunella shout angrily at the library ghost and the library ghost shout joyfully back. It's very difficult to win an argument with a ghost, especially the ghost of a librarian, because librarians know everything.

Then Alfie suddenly realised that he couldn't smell Featherlegs's breath any more or hear her slobbering.

He opened his eyes in time to see something flicker down the hall. It was too big for a bee and too round for a dragonfly. It swooped down and landed on Alfie's chest.

The Eye-Spy! The green bloodshot eye swivelled and fixed on him. Long green leafy ears (a bit crushed now) waggled delicately.

Alfie heard the faint voice of his Aunt Zita.

'Alfie, listen and we'll get you out. Have you any All-Purpose Witching Powder with you?'

'In my pocket,' murmured Alfie. 'But I can't reach it.'

'Why not?'

'I can only move my eyes.'

'And your mouth,' said Zita's voice snippily. 'Just try. All you need to do is take the lid off the bottle; the spell will do the rest.'

Featherlegs had spun her web so tightly around him that Alfie despaired of reaching the bottle in his anorak pocket. But he wriggled and thrashed and managed to get hold of the bottle and push the lid off.

'It's open!' he puffed.

'Great!' said Zita's voice. 'Now repeat these words after me, Alfie.

'Spiders are nice; spiders are good,
If they crunch flies as they should!
But some eat children and that ain't right,
They wrap 'em and spin 'em up all tight!
If one of these bugs hooks you for its tea,
Shout this spell and you'll be FREE!'

Alfie repeated the words and watched as the web that had bound him so tightly transformed before his eyes. Instead of Featherlegs's extra-strong spider thread, he was wrapped up in . . . slimy spaghetti!

There were some loud bangs and fizzes down the corridor. The Eye-Spy turned and flew off in their direction.

Alfie sat up and pulled away the spaghetti. Featherlegs was nowhere to be seen; Prunella was distracted arguing with the library ghost. He could go back to the old plan and try to pinch the golden key and turn Prunella into a butter dish. Or pinch the golden key, minimise the Head Witch, trap her in a glass and flush her down the toilet.

Or he could find a nice cupboard and hide in it until all this was over.

Well, what would you do?

The HUGE GREAT BIG LOUD BANG was heard by everyone.

(Everyone talked about it for months afterwards because it was the loudest EVER.)

Granny Fagan, who was in the village fighting Mrs Mention's gingerbread army, heard it.

Calypso and Zita, who were lost in the secret passage, heard it.

Alfie, who was deciding what to do, heard it.

Gertrude had just cast a very big and difficult spell. It was a spell to bring the house to life. And now Switherbroom Hall was fighting back against the intruders!

The curtains wound themselves around the hidden guards. The chandeliers crashed down on the surprised guards' heads. Ornaments came flying through the air – guards were set upon by flying vases and hopping candlesticks, whizzing kitchen knives and thrashing tea trays. The guards that had turned themselves into furniture quickly changed back, only to be changed into other objects by the witches that came running through the rooms throwing green powder and shouting spells.

Have you ever been in a witch fight? I hope not. Well, this is what it's like: loud pops, green smoke, funny smells, sudden flashes.

Stand in the wrong place and you might find yourself turned into a stone, a stick or a stinky cat poo.

Only saying.

Alfie stepped towards Prunella, silver bottle in hand and spell at the ready.

Prunella had her back to him. Her face was pressed against the library door and she was roaring rudeness. The library ghost had disappeared.

Alfie could see the chain around her neck that held the golden key.

He sprinkled some green powder in his hand.

But then he realised he didn't have the snips!

He could tug hard – her necklace might break. Then quick with the powder and spell! But this was bound to go wrong!

Perhaps inspired by the pops and whizzes and bangs coming from the other parts of the house, Prunella suddenly stepped back and threw a green thunderbolt at the locked door.

CRASH!

Alfie was blown along the corridor.

And another thunderbolt—

CRASH!

And another—

CRASH!

As the smoke settled, Alfie could see a tiny hole in the door, no bigger than a grape.

Prunella saw it too. 'Featherlegs, I need your fangs. Get over here and gnaw this hole bigger,' she ordered.

No Featherlegs came forward.

The Head Witch looked around.

There was no Featherlegs, only Alfie lying in the corridor with a handful of green powder.

Outside there was mayhem.

Mrs Mention's gingerbread army had marched to Switherbroom Hall, try as the witches might to stop them!

The biscuit soldiers were fast, with teeth like razors.

If you smashed them in two, they could join together again!

If you knocked off a limb, they grew another – like starfish!

The Familiars snapped at them.

The witches swiped at them.

Granny Fagan circled the battalions of soldiers on her motorbike, throwing bottles of All-Purpose Witching Powder at them and shouting an exploding spell. Until the air was thick with clouds of sparkling sugary dust.

Behind the gingerbread army clanked Mrs Mention; she had made armour from baking trays and was beating two pan lids together in a terrifying manner.

'Hooray for the Head Witch!' she roared. 'PRUNELLA FOREVER!'

Calypso and Zita had found an open door. A way out of the secret-passage maze!

It was Calypso's idea to follow the trail Featherlegs had made dragging Alfie along, figuring that it would lead them to an exit.

They stepped out of the passage. All around them were the sounds of witches fighting, the bangs, pops and whizzes of spells being made.

'Quick, to the library!' Zita dashed off down the hallway.

There was a CRASH! and a FRIZZZZZZ!

And Calypso was nowhere to be seen.

Prunella held out her hand.

Alfie handed over the bottle of All-Purpose Witching Powder.

'And the rest!' growled Prunella.

Followed by the jar of Enemy Minimising Powder.

Now he had no chance.

No spells.

No magic.

Nothing to fight Prunella with!

There was no way he could take the golden key now.

He needed that key as much as Prunella, it seemed, needed to get in the door. She had seen, with a howl of temper, that the hole she had blasted in the library door had fixed itself.

The door was as good as new!

But what if Prunella thought she could get through the door by *giving* him the key?

An idea bubbled up in Alfie's mind.

'I think you're fibbing, Blackstack.'

'I never fib,' said Alfie.

Prunella looked doubtful. She knocked loudly on the library door. 'Get out here, ghost. I want to talk to you.'

The library ghost drifted out, nose in the air. 'Someone around here really ought to learn some manners.'

'That boy,' Prunella pointed at Alfie, 'says that my golden key will open this door.'

The hint of a smile appeared on the library ghost's face.

Prunella continued, 'Only, the golden key must be turned by a Blackstack, because if a Morrow tries to open the door, the key will melt or whatever.'

'Perhaps you should give the boy the golden key then,' said the ghost.

Prunella took off her necklace. 'I've never had so much trouble getting in a door! And it's not even to somewhere fun – just a dusty old LIBRARY!'

The Head Witch handed Alfie the golden key.

Then this happened:

Granny Fagan roared past Mrs Mention and pushed her with her broom into a flowerbed.

Gertrude and her band of witches, a canteen of flying cutlery, a flock of angry teacups and a furious piano chased the last of Prunella's guards out of the house. All the witches cheered and ran up the stairs to the library.

Featherlegs, scuttling back to the library, dragging a web-wrapped Calypso behind her, came to a halt in the corridor.

Zita, running after Featherlegs with a bottle of All-Purpose Witching Powder open and ready, stopped too.

Alfie stood outside the library with Prunella's golden key in his hand.

The library ghost loosened his bonnet strings.

Out spun the snow globe. It hovered in the air before Alfie.

The keyhole glowed green – Alfie put the key in.

'NO!' shouted Prunella, a look of alarm on her face.

Alfie turned the key.

*

The HUGE GREAT BIG BRIGHT FLASH was seen by everyone.

(Everyone talked about it for months afterwards because it was the brightest EVER.)

The snow globe spun, faster and faster.

Rude noises erupted from it.

And then a loud giggle.

'NOVA!' cried Calypso, recognising her little sister's laugh.

'Quiet, dinnertime!' Featherlegs hissed, and started to pull Calypso away from the chaos. She was very hungry now – these meals had been dangled before her for days!

'Get off me, spider!' fumed Calypso. 'Let me go. I have to save my sister.'

Then Calypso remembered what Zita had said – that Nova had put *herself* in there.

Calypso addressed the snow globe. 'This is your BIG SISTER speaking.'

The snow globe stopped spinning and hung in the air.

'Come out of that snow globe at once! You've been very naughty putting yourself in there!'

There was a puff of green smoke.

When the smoke cleared, a little girl was sitting cross-legged on the floor.

'Nova!' cried Calypso.

Featherlegs, not to be done out of another snack, scuttled off, dragging Calypso behind her.

But Nova had seen them and her eyes glowed green. 'BAD SPIDER! COME HERE!'

265

The little girl pointed at Featherlegs and Featherlegs was gone.

'What have you done with my Familiar, you brat?' raged Prunella.

Nova opened her hand. Featherlegs, spider-sized, crawled across her palm.

The web that had bound Calypso disappeared – she was free again! She got to her feet and rushed towards her sister.

Then she stopped.

The snow globe had started spinning again and sparking green fire.

It was gathering speed.

And growing.

It grew to the size of a grapefruit.

Then the size of a melon . . .

Then the size of a beach ball . . .

Then bigger than a beach ball . . .

Then it stopped spinning. A ladder dropped out of the bottom and down climbed a small figure.

The imp was no taller than Nova and dressed all in conker-brown velvet. On his feet he wore shiny black shoes with silver buckles.

He had a freckled, upturned nose, huge yellow eyes and a shock of bright green hair . . . and a big smile.

He looked very handsome indeed.

'IMP!' shouted Nova with glee.

Prunella turned to run.

A golden net appeared in the imp's hand. He threw it over the departing Head Witch, who screamed with fury as she began to tangle and trip.

King Wormfrall took a scroll of paper from inside his smart jacket. He unrolled it.

He nodded to Alfie, who read it out loud.

'PRUNELLA MORROW HED WICH
YOU HVE
CUT DOWN OUR TREE
DESTORYD OUR HOME
TURND PEPLE INTO STICKS AND STONES
PUT ME IN THIS SNO GLOB!'

The imp shook the scroll and the letters rearranged themselves.

'I KING WORMFRALL SENTINCE YOU
PRUNELLA MORROW
AN YOR FAMILIAR FEATHERLEGS
TO LIFE IN PRISON
IN THIS SNO GLB.'

'You can't do that!' sneered Prunella. 'I'm the Head Witch! And there's no magic strong enough to put me in that snow globe!'

The imp king looked at Nova and the little girl laughed.

Nova opened her fist and looked down at Featherlegs in her hand. 'Bad bug!'

Then Nova looked up at Prunella. 'Bad girl, BAD, BAD GIRL!'

'Look at Nova's eyes!' exclaimed Gertrude.

Everyone watched in amazement.

Nova's eyes shone, brighter and brighter, greener and greener.

She sang a merry song – it might have been something to do with squirrels; nobody quite caught the words.

King Wormfrall hummed along, tapping a shiny black shoe.

Prunella, tangled up in Wormfrall's net, looked on aghast.

When her song was finished, Nova clapped her hands.

Alfie grimaced. Squished spider, surely?

But when Nova held up her open palms, there was nothing there.

And Wormfrall's net was empty too!

From the snow globe came a piercing shriek followed by a loud angry babble.

Then the snow globe began to shrink again – beach ball – melon – grapefruit – dusty old doorknob.

The snow globe hung in the air.

Everyone moved forward.

The blizzard inside began to clear.

And there was a white plane in miniature. Prunella ran up the steps sobbing, Featherlegs scuttling after her. The door of the plane slammed behind them. And then the words appeared:

SHOW'S OVER

King Wormfrall smiled. He bowed to the audience, blew Nova a kiss and was gone. And with him the scroll of paper vanished, in a puff of green smoke, as magic messages often do.

'Bye, bye, KING!' said Nova.

CHAPTER 28

Summer Ends

After any great party comes the tidying up.

Many of the witches had stayed on at Switherbroom Hall. These were exciting times – forming a brand-new council and electing a new Head Witch. Zita's name was at the top of the list, of course.

No one gave a second thought to Prunella Morrow or Featherlegs. Prunella's remaining guards (who hadn't been chased away or turned into sticks) changed out of their uniforms and gave their caps away to the younger witches as souvenirs. For days to come everyone enjoyed the marshmallow helicopters.

Switherbroom Hall was soon patched up and set right with the help of a spot of magic. In the forest, flashes of bright green were seen and laughter was heard. The imps were back, it was said. The trees were delighted and produced a firework show of red and yellow autumn leaves to celebrate.

The villagers, who had changed from plants back into people, remembered little of their afternoon at the circus. Now and again the odd detail came back to them, when they were asleep perhaps, or day-dreaming: dancing crocodiles and rolling dice, flying vacuum cleaners and bright green flashes.

Mrs Mention, it was said, had gone on a permanent vacation, somewhere small and self-contained with plenty of windows. Two newcomers to the village had taken over the tea room, stringing up a painted banner.

Bodkin and O'Malley
Fine Teas and Magical Pastries
Bewitching Cream Cakes a speciality
EVERYONE WELCOME!

The villagers of Little Snoddington now enjoyed their cream teas alongside the peculiar guests from Switherbroom Hall, who would bring along the strangest assortments of pets. Toads snoozed under tea cosies and weasels curled up in laps. Cats hunted napkins and bats swung happily from the picture rail. Now that Mrs Mention was gone the circus folk were greeted gladly in the tea room. Soon it was rumoured that Granny Fagan had been seen smiling over her teacup at Mrs Vicar, and Mrs Vicar had been seen nodding back.

Did Alfie put a drop of Gentle Friendliness Tonic in the teapots after all? Shh, I'm not telling.

The summer had ended, as all things end, of course. And with the end of summer came the return of Mr Fingerhut from his fishing trip. He had been seen walking down the high street, putting down his suitcase and unlocking the door to his dusty shop.

He had put his tatty old stuffed weasel up behind the counter and turned the 'Closed' sign to 'Open'.

All these small things meant one big thing: it was time for the circus to leave town.

★

Moley and Hester put a few extra cakes on Alfie's order, for he was entertaining a visitor from out of town: Clarice the childminder, who brought with her a string of babies, all holding hands and toddling behind her like bewildered baby chicks.

Nova looked quite grown up compared to Clarice's rock babies. She climbed up on the chair next to Alfie's. She loved Alfie best; next to Calypso, of course.

Alfie smiled down at her and her eyes glowed green.

Since her stay in the snow globe Nova's eyes often turned from blue to green – a marvellous bright green. Especially when she was happy.

'I knew you'd settle in all right, Alfie!' smiled Clarice. 'And it's lovely to meet you, Calypso. I've heard so much about Alfie's *best ever friend*.'

Alfie reddened. Calypso grinned.

Clarice nudged Alfie. 'You write such brilliant letters, I feel like I know this place so well.'

Calypso glanced at Alfie. 'Not *too* well, I hope?'

He pulled a face.

'And you've found stuff to do here, Alfie?' Clarice asked, popping a spoonful of chocolate pudding into a baby's open mouth.

'Oh yes, there's stuff to do here.'

'Not too quiet?'

'No, not too quiet.'

'And you like it?'

Alfie smiled. 'Every day is sort of magical.'

'That's great news! Now, before I forget, this came to the old house for you.' Clarice rummaged in her handbag and handed Alfie an envelope.

'It's a bit of a mystery, to be honest.' Clarice paused. 'This letter was dated and sent to London weeks *after* . . . your father, leaky boat, rocky island, rough seas.'

All of a sudden there were butterflies in Alfie's tummy and a leaping of his heart.

Could this mean that his father was still somehow *alive*?

Alfie looked at the envelope.

It had a smear of chocolate pudding on the corner. The writing on the front was definitely his father's, full of impatient loops and irritated dots.

273

FOR MASTER ALFRED BLACKSTACK
ON THE OCCASION OF HIS TENTH
BIRTHDAY

Alfie would think about the mystery of how his father's letter was sent later. Right now he would just see what was inside.

'It's your birthday, Alfie!' cried Calypso, catching sight of the card.

Alfie nodded. 'Just gone.'

'You didn't tell me, you toad!' exclaimed Calypso, punching Alfie's arm.

'I forgot! We were sort of busy.'

'Well, I'm throwing you a birthday party,' announced Calypso. 'Circus style!'

Alfie laughed. He opened the envelope. Inside was a birthday card with a picture of an owl on it. *It would be a bird*, he thought.

And then he felt sad for his dad and for his mum.

Nova put a sticky hand on his arm and he smiled at her.

'There was something inside the card, Alfie. It's fallen out.' Calypso handed him a small green ticket.

Alfie looked at it. The ticket was edged with drawings of all manner of birds, animals and insects.

THIS COUPON ENTITLES THE BEARER
TO ONE *FAMILIAR*

N.B. One creature per voucher
Not to be traded for vacuum cleaners
For use in participating shops only

Alfie turned over the ticket and was only half surprised to find Mr Fingerhut's Fun Emporium was the single participating shop.

Alfie returned to his birthday card and read the words that his father had dashed there.

Alfred,
   Happy Birthday and all that.
   SEE ME about the enclosed (there's something you ought to know about our family, being ten and all that).
   Best wishes and all that.
   Your father,
   Phineas Blackstack

'Thank you, Clarice,' said Alfie politely.

Clarice smiled at him. 'I hope it's something you wanted.'

Alfie nodded. 'Yes, I think it is.'

★

Alfie and Calypso stood outside the tea room waving goodbye to Clarice and the babies. Back they would go to London – to the noise and people and pigeons, the black cabs and red buses – a world away from Little Snoddington.

'I think my father wanted me to know magic after all,' said Alfie. He handed Calypso the green ticket.

'A Familiar?' She looked excited. 'You'll get a weasel like the other gentlemen witches.'

'I will not. I'll get a newt; I'll call him Newton.'

'Trust you!' Calypso laughed. Then she was serious. 'Why do you think our parents kept magic from us?'

'Because it's a bit dangerous?' suggested Alfie.

'So is climbing cliffs and taming lions and swinging on a trapeze – but our parents did all of that.'

'Your parents had a trapeze act?'

Calypso nodded. 'Mum did. Who do you think I learnt it from?'

Alfie and Calypso wandered down to Blackstacks' Chemist's Shop. Nova walked in the middle holding one of Alfie's hands and one of Calypso's. She no longer needed the pushchair now, only sometimes, when she was tired.

'Are you a bit sad to see Clarice go?' asked Calypso.

'A bit,' Alfie paused. 'But I'll be sadder to see you go.' He squeezed Nova's hand. 'And this little rotter!'

Nova laughed.

'It's sad when friends leave, isn't it?' said Calypso. 'But we'll be back at Christmas time. Gertrude has been speaking to Dad about a festive circus extravaganza!'

'That's months away!'

'I know, Alfie. But we'll phone and write too.'

'Bat post!' smiled Alfie.

Calypso laughed. 'Alfie, you will always, always be my best friend.'

Alfie felt a tremendous happiness bubbling up inside him. He could hardly speak. 'Really, honestly?'

'Really, honestly!'

Alfie felt like whooping and shouting down the street and telling Calypso that she was his best friend ever in a million years and he hoped they would have more adventures, even dangerous ones involving everyday magic, because you can be scared and brave at the same time, and when you have a best friend everything is all right with the world!

Instead Alfie said, 'Oh, cool.'

Calypso smiled. She knew exactly what Alfie meant.

Rafferty was asleep, belly-up, in the sunny window of Blackstacks' Chemist's Shop. He woke when he heard Alfie and Calypso and Nova arrive and went to purr around their ankles.

Gertrude gave the children a hug and called for Zita, who emerged from her mixing room. Zita wore an apron and goggles and an absent-minded expression. She was working hard to find a way to reverse the Forever Spell – inspired by Prunella.

Magnus, hanging upside down on the coat stand, wrapped his wings more tightly about himself. He still hadn't quite forgiven Calypso for kissing him.

Gertrude lifted down a jar marked:

CAT-FLAVOURED LOLLIES

Orange and Ginger
Contains: No Cats

Nova pulled out a lolly and held it up: a perfect bright-orange copy of Rafferty's face, just one of Gertrude's brand-new bestsellers, along with her Ever-Changing Hair Dye. Many of the villagers now had hair like Gertrude: one day green, another day purple, tomorrow – who knows!

Gertrude smiled at the children. 'Where are you all off to now?'

Alfie glanced at Calypso. 'Thought we'd call in to Mr Fingerhut's shop.'

Gertrude nodded. 'But watch out, some of his stock can be a bit . . . *unpredictable*.'

Alfie glanced at the snow globe on a shelf behind the counter. It was attached to the wall with a special golden chain, just to be on the safe side. Snow globes, after all, are known to go wandering.

Today there was a thick blizzard swirling inside.

Nova wandered up and tapped the snow globe with her lolly. 'Hello, little spider!'

The blizzard kept swirling. Although Alfie was sure he could glimpse a line of black glittering eyes just behind.

'No spider today,' said Zita. 'And Prunella is in a bad mood again. She's been muttering all morning.'

'On a good day, she'll help me with my crossword,' Gertrude said. 'Although she often gives me the wrong answers on purpose!'

278

'Bad girl!' said Nova.

'Yes, she is,' nodded Gertrude, her face suddenly serious. She glanced at Calypso.

Calypso bit her lip and looked away.

Alfie felt sad for his friend.

He knew that Calypso had been talking to Gertrude about her mum. About what might have happened to Ursula and how Prunella might have been involved.

But Prunella, trapped and angry and wickeder than ever, was saying nothing.

Would they ever solve the mystery of Ursula Morrow's disappearance?

Or the mystery of how it was possible for Phineas Blackstack to write and send a letter to Alfie days after he failed to return in his boat?

Alfie would talk to his aunts later about the growing feeling that his father might be out there somewhere, alive. He glanced at his friend. Her mother would likely not come back and Calypso's face said that she knew this. It didn't seem right for Alfie to be celebrating his own spark of hope.

'I've been wondering where Mr Fingerhut got the snow globe in the first place,' said Alfie. 'If Prunella imprisoned the imp inside, then wasn't the snow globe hers to begin with?'

'Magical snow globes get about, you should know that!' said Gertrude.

'I did ask Mr Fingerhut,' Alfie added.

'And?'

'He just walked off talking into his beard.'

Gertrude nodded. 'Sounds about right, Alfie.'

'Is Mr Fingerhut a witch?' Calypso asked. 'After all, he has a beard and a weasel—'

'Watch out for that weasel!' exclaimed Gertrude.

'So, he's *magical*? I mean, he gave Alfie a magical snow globe.'

Gertrude looked thoughtful. 'When it comes to Ignatius Fingerhut, I think it's probably best not to ask too many questions, Calypso.'

Zita scoffed. 'He just likes stirring up trouble, the old trickster!'

'That's as may be,' said Gertrude wisely. 'But he always has some kind of plan.' She smiled at the children. 'See how well things worked out. The imp is free, the Head Witch is gone and Granny Fagan and Mrs Vicar are the best of friends!'

'I wouldn't go that far!' laughed Alfie.

Gertrude held out the jar again. The label had changed and now read:

BAT-FLAVOURED LOLLIES
Liquorice and Cola
Contains: No Bats

Alfie and Calypso and Nova rambled down the quiet village road. They were silent but for the slurping of their lollipops.

'I think Mr Fingerhut's a witch or a wizard or whatever,' Calypso announced.

'Course he is!'

'Are you going to get a Familiar, Alfie?'

Alfie took out the green ticket and looked at it. Magic was still strange to him; he wondered if it always would be. But he was getting used to this new, peculiar sort of brilliant life.

He lived in a big draughty house with no electricity stuck out in a forest, with two aunts he never knew he had, who were actually witches, who ran a chemist's shop in a village where *sometimes* not much happened.

Gone was the life he knew: his old house, his old school, London. And in its place? Somewhere he felt he could belong, with people he could belong to. Which is everything anyone needs after all.

He pocketed the green ticket. 'Maybe I should get a Familiar.'

'Might be fun,' nodded Calypso.

'What about you? Wouldn't you like one too though?'

Calypso smiled. 'Maybe I'll get a ticket for my birthday. I'll see next month!'

'You can have my ticket,' said Alfie shyly. 'If you want it.'

Calypso grinned. 'You sap!'

Mr Fingerhut glanced up from behind his counter. His shop was no less dusty or cluttered than last time. The stuffed weasel sneered down from the shelf behind him.

Alfie was certain it moved. 'Keep an eye on that weasel, Nova!' he whispered.

281

Nova sat down on the floor and watched the weasel.

Mr Fingerhut pointed at her. 'She had blue eyes.'

'They're a lot greener since her stay in the snow globe,' said Calypso, a little snappily.

Mr Fingerhut looked shifty. 'All's well that ends well.' He cleared his throat. 'You have a ticket, Alfred Blackstack, that entitles you to a Familiar?'

Alfie fished for the ticket in his pocket. 'How did you know?'

'Turned ten, didn't you?'

Alfie nodded.

'So, you'd like to see what Familiars I have in stock?'

'Maybe I'll wait until Calypso can get one too.'

Mr Fingerhut turned to Calypso. 'When's your birthday?'

'Next month.'

'And you'll be ten?'

Calypso nodded.

Mr Fingerhut glanced at his weasel and then he scratched his beard awhile.

'All right,' he said. 'Bring your ticket in when you get it. You can both pick your Familiars today.'

Mr Fingerhut rummaged under the counter and brought out a dusty photograph album and a coin.

'Who calls?' he said. 'Heads or tails?'

'You call, Alfie,' urged Calypso.

'Heads.'

Mr Fingerhut tossed the coin. 'It's tails: first pick to Calypso Morrow.'

'Calypso *Fagan*, if you please,' said Calypso.

Mr Fingerhut pushed the photograph album towards her. 'They're all in there. Insects, mammals, reptiles, birds, marine creatures – although those are only for seafaring witches.'

'What are "miscellaneous"?' asked Calypso, pointing to the heading.

'Mostly rocks; some like a Familiar that's easy to keep.'

Calypso let out a delighted cry. 'Him!' she laughed, tapping the photograph. 'Definitely him, what do you think, Alfie?'

It was a picture of a huge shaggy dog. Alfie read the words printed underneath aloud.

'Name: Finbar Feeney
Type: Canis lupus familiaris, *Irish Wolfhound*
Qualities: Intelligent, loyal, brave'

'All right, over to you, Master Blackstack.'

Mr Fingerhut slid the album towards Alfie, who accidentally dropped it.

'Sorry!' Alfie picked up the album and put it on the counter.

'A photograph has fallen out,' said Calypso. She scooped it up off the floor and looked at it. 'Oh, hilarious!'

Alfie went to open the album. 'I'll put it back.'

'Wait right there!' bellowed Mr Fingerhut. 'Your Familiar is picked.'

Mr Fingerhut pointed to the photograph in Calypso's

hand. It was of a bright green bird with a red beak and orange eyes.

'But I didn't pick it,' said Alfie. 'The photograph fell out when I dropped the album.'

'Same difference.' Mr Fingerhut rummaged under his counter again and brought out a long scroll of yellowing paper. He unwound it and read:

'Rule 157(a)
If during the choosing of the Familiar the album is dropped by the choosee and a photograph falls out, THAT shall be the chosen Familiar.'

Alfie stared at the picture. 'A parrot?'

'A parakeet actually,' said Calypso.

Mr Fingerhut flicked through the album. Then he turned it around for Alfie to see, stabbing with his finger at the page where a picture was missing.

Alfie stuck the photograph back in and read aloud:

'Name: Doris Florida
Type: Psittacula krameri, Ring-necked parakeet
Qualities: Noisy, daring, jester'

'Oh no,' groaned Alfie. 'Noisy and daring?'

Mr Fingerhut smiled. 'Might be just what you need, Master Blackstack.' He glanced up at the weasel. 'Although a weasel is the usual choice, of course.'

'For gentlemen witches,' added Calypso under her breath.

'Beatrice, dear, would you be so kind as to bring in the Familiars?' said Mr Fingerhut.

The weasel hopped down from its stand and slipped out the back door of the shop.

Nova laughed.

'I knew that weasel was real!' exclaimed Alfie.

They waited. Mr Fingerhut stroked his beard. Calypso shuffled from foot to foot impatiently and Nova drew on the dusty floor with her lollipop stick.

Alfie wondered what he was going to do with a loud-beaked, mad-capped parakeet.

The weasel ran into the room followed by a dog the size of a horse and a beautiful green bird.

The dog dropped to a play bow, his tail wagging madly. Calypso and Nova fell on him squealing.

The bird flapped over to the counter and landed. It waggled one foot, then the other and then it winked at Alfie.

'HERE COMES TROUBLE!' it squawked.

'I hope not,' sighed Alfie.

Mr Fingerhut turned to Nova. 'I'm afraid you can't have a Familiar until you are bigger, little witch.'

Nova offered him her lollipop stick.

Mr Fingerhut smiled and his eyes went crinkly and he didn't seem stern at all.

'But you can still have something to take home,' said the old man, and wandered off into the corner of the shop.

He returned carrying a small wooden box and put it on the counter.

'It's an old-fashioned camera!' said Alfie.

Mr Fingerhut set the box down on the counter. 'It's a magic lantern, of the *most* magical kind.'

Nova drew near and put down her lollipop stick. Mr Fingerhut helped her climb up on a chair so that she could reach the counter. Then he showed her how to look through the eyehole at the front of the box.

Alfie glanced at Calypso. 'Should we let her have it?' he said. 'I mean, is it a good idea? You know what happened last time.'

Calypso laughed. 'That's exactly why it's a good idea, Alfie Blackstack.'

And Alfie laughed too.

Acknowledgements

Huge thanks (always!) to my agent, the magical Sue Armstrong, who makes all stories possible. To the brilliant team at C&W, especially Emma Finn, Clare Conville, Jake Smith-Bosanquet and Katie Greenstreet – thank you. To the marvellous Luke Speed from Curtis Brown who always cheers me on – I so value your support and encouragement.

To my wise and wonderful editor, Jo Dingley, thank you for helping me to bring Alfie's world to life. Special thanks also to Megan Reid and Ailsa Bathgate for all your insights and to Jenny Glencross for your early advice. Big gratitude to the Canongate Family; Francis Bickmore, Jenny Fry, Jamie Byng, Lucy Zhou, Vicki Watson, Vicki Rutherford, Jamie Norman, Alan Trotter and the team. Thanks go to Beatriz Castro for the fabulous illustrations.

To Nova, thank you for letting me borrow your wonderful name. I really hope that you and your big sister Pagan enjoy this story, especially the cats and bats and crocodiles!

To my family and friends – you know who you are – massive gratitude. To my small one grown big, Eva – thank you for inspiring this story all those years ago.